# Maximum Wrist Snap

My voice. The voice I used to say over and over *"Everything's great. Great, really, fine, fine."* I've said it so many times that things either have to start going great, or I cut the crap.

And the one thing that had always been great, the one last thing I knew for sure about—hitting a baseball—was being sucked down the same drain as my brother's life. I'd never hit the ball again, thanks to his stupid, stupid, stupid cancer—

I picked up the stick and swung hard. That hockey stick flamed past the edge of the closet. Bashed the glass into fifty pieces. The guy in the mirror never stood a chance.

I dropped the stick on the floor. Good thing Tom's already dying. Good thing. Otherwise I'd have to kill him.

# OTHER BOOKS YOU MAY ENJOY

# HOLDING at THIRD

**LINDA ZINNEN**

PUFFIN BOOKS

PUFFIN BOOKS

Published by the Penguin Group

Penguin Young Readers Group,

345 Hudson Street, New York, New York 10014, U.S.A.

Penguin Group (Canada), 90 Eglinton Avenue East, Suite 700, Toronto, Ontario, Canada M4P 2Y3

(a division of Pearson Penguin Canada Inc.)

Penguin Books Ltd, 80 Strand, London WC2R 0RL, England

Penguin Ireland, 25 St Stephen's Green, Dublin 2, Ireland (a division of Penguin Books Ltd)

Penguin Group (Australia), 250 Camberwell Road, Camberwell, Victoria 3124, Australia

(a division of Pearson Australia Group Pty Ltd)

Penguin Books India Pvt Ltd, 11 Community Centre, Panchsheel Park,

New Delhi - 110 017, India

Penguin Group (NZ), Cnr Airborne and Rosedale Roads, Albany, Auckland 1310, New Zealand

(a division of Pearson New Zealand Ltd)

Penguin Books (South Africa) (Pty) Ltd, 24 Sturdee Avenue, Rosebank,

Johannesburg 2196, South Africa

Registered Offices: Penguin Books Ltd, 80 Strand, London WC2R 0RL, England

First published in the United States of America by Dutton Children's Books,

a division of Penguin Young Readers Group, 2004

Published by Puffin Books, a division of Penguin Young Readers Group, 2006

3 5 7 9 10 8 6 4 2

THE LIBRARY OF CONGRESS HAS CATALOGED THE DUTTON EDITION AS FOLLOWS:

Zinnen, Linda.

Holding at third / by Linda Zinnen.—1st ed.

p. cm.

Summary: When thirteen-year-old Matt's older brother Tom moves to a different
hospital to receive a "treatment of last resort" for his cancer, Matt tries to adjust to
a new home and school, a new baseball team, and his feelings about his brother.

ISBN: 0-525-47163-4 (hc)

[ 1. Brothers—Fiction. 2. Cancer—Patients—Fiction. 3. Sick—Fiction.
4. Baseball—Fiction. 5. Moving, Household—Fiction.]

I. Title.

PZ7.Z6545Ho 2004

[Fic]—dc22  2003049272

Puffin Books ISBN 0-14-240554-X

Printed in the United States of America

**FOR GREG,
WHO LOVES THIS BOOK**

# CONTENTS

# Holding at Third

# 1

## THE BAINTER FAMILY
## AUTOMATIC FIELDING MACHINE

**"SEE?** It's gonna be great," said Matt Bainter. He stood on the porch and looked at the sun sinking behind the trees across the road. "Coach Pangbourn called last night. The Ohio Athletics Board granted me a waiver to play for Upper West. Due to circumstances and stuff."

"You're ditching us. Gonna live in a mansion and play center field for Upper West Bexley." Ross Berg shook his head sadly. "A team that never makes the playoffs."

"A team we always beat," added Tyler Smith.

"Yeah, what were they last season?" asked Ross all innocent, like he didn't already know. "We won state, and they finished what? Fifth?"

"Fourth," said Matt. He shoved Ross off the porch and into his mom's flower bed. "They finished fourth."

Ross picked up a wet dirt clod and threw it at Matt's head. He missed. "'Course, with your bat, they're headed for third. Definitely."

"Maybe even second," said Ty. Ross just laughed and threw another clod. Ty caught it and threw it back. It hit Ross square in the stomach and exploded all over his shirt.

"Try catching with your hands," advised Matt. "Works better."

Ross brushed at the mud. "So. You're going up tomorrow, huh? You and your mom and Tom?"

"Yep," said Matt.

"Your brother's last treatment."

"Yep."

Ty shoved Matt off the porch. "It won't be bad. Tom will do okay."

"Tom will do great," said Matt. "This one last thing. Then he's all set." The sun was low enough to shine in his eyes. He closed them.

"Matt?" said Ross quietly. "You okay?"

Matt thought about how long it had been since he'd been okay. Long enough that it made him feel tired and dizzy, trying to remember the feeling. He opened his eyes. "I'll be home in time for play-offs."

Ross looked him over, but all he said was, "Sure. Meantime, my dad bought me this phone card. A hundred twenty minutes. I'll call ya."

Matt didn't want to think about it, so he jerked his head toward Ty. Ross grinned. They leaped onto the porch and threw Ty into the dirt.

Tom's dog, Axle—part shepherd, part collie, and pure ball hound—must have heard Tyler yell. He loped around the corner of the house with a tennis ball in his mouth. He dropped the ball on Ty's foot, then snarled hopefully.

"Hey, Axle, how 'bout you come and play center field for us while Matt's gone?" said Ross. "We could use a smart dog on defense."

"He'd play harder than Todd Striker ever will," said Matt. It hurt thinking about leaving Amesville's center field in the hands of Todd, the human lard bucket.

Tyler picked up Axle's ball. "Todd stinks. You should stay."

Ross glanced at Matt. "Nah. He's got his mind up there already."

Matt shoved Ross off the porch again. "My mind is on the season. Tom's gonna do great. Upper West is gonna have a fine run to state. End of story." It was getting hard to say "Yep, yep, everything's working out great." He wondered how much longer he could keep it up.

"Oh, ho ho. Upper West at *state,*" snorted Ty as he threw the ball over the house. The ball sailed over the chimney. Axle charged up the front steps, leaped onto the porch railing, and hurtled over the gutters on the slanted porch roof. Matt could hear Axle's claws ripping through the shingles as he disappeared over the roofline and skied down the back slope, off the roof, after the ball. Ross shook his head.

"That is one insane dog," he said. "When are you going to teach him to go around the house?"

Matt shrugged. "I can't teach him nothing. He's Tom's dog, mostly."

Matt's mom came charging out of the house. "You boys get out of my flower bed and stop tempting that poor, brainless dog to go over the roof," she bellowed. "Or your butts will be up there nailing down new shingles!" Axle trotted around the corner, gnashing the ball with his teeth. "Take him in the backyard and play decent!"

Matt grabbed Axle's collar and yanked him to the backyard, to the homemade ball field complete with a dirt pitcher's mound and blue car mats for bases. The pine tree outside his and Tom's bedroom marked the right-field foul line; left field ended by the woods. Matt knew every inch by heart.

He wrestled the ball away from Axle. The boys spread out and threw it around a little. Axle tore around the grass, growling and snapping, crazy to get his teeth on the ball again as the three of them ran and threw and naturally drifted into their field positions—Tyler on the mound; Ross crouched low behind home plate; and Matt roaming center field, controlling the outfield for Tyler, working in close to catch Ross's throw to second.

And everything that had been awkward and scary and wrecked about the last couple of months just didn't matter for a while. Ty horsed around, spinning a high throw over his shoulder in the general direction of left field. The ball took a bad bounce on a molehill and skidded into short center. Matt body-blocked Axle's Kamikaze lunge for the grounder and ended up face-down in the dirt. He got a noseful of the smell of baseball rising out of the muddy spring grass. That smell was powerful, promising. Another season as center-field cannon, even if he was holding on to nothing better than Axle's dog-spit tennis ball. Even if he was holding on to the sad fact that no matter how good the hospital stuff finally turned out for his older brother, Tom, he personally was going to be stuck playing center field for the league's fourth-place team.

Fourth place. And that was in a *good* year. Matt frowned as he wiped the mud off the ball.

"Go home, Axle," he said. "Beat the throw. Git!"

Axle raced across the infield. Matt fired the ball over the plate to Ross, who tagged Axle out. Ross pegged the ball back to Tyler. Tyler stared down at that dirty tennis ball like he'd never seen anything like it in his life. Matt held his breath. Here it was. The moment had come. Sure enough, Ty coiled into his stance. The ball flamed over the plate. Ross caught it with a bite-me grin on his face.

Baseball. He was looking at baseball. Matt let out his breath.

He watched Ross and Ty, that bullet rhythm they shared as pitcher and catcher. Axle raced between mound and home, leaping for the ball. Ty's pitches were too quick. Axle couldn't lay a tooth on them. Drove him ape crazy, finally. The dog attacked Ross, knocked him flat on his butt, and snatched the tennis ball out of his hand.

Matt grinned. He trotted over to the garden shed and scrounged around. He lobbed Tyler every ball that had ended up on a winter haven in the shed—a couple of baseballs, an orange Wiffle ball, a bunch of golf balls, softballs, more tennis balls, even a partially flattened soccer ball. Ty lined them up arrow-straight next to his right foot while Matt took a quick look through the junk—under the garden hose, behind the rakes and snow shovels—and found his old wooden bat.

Crap, he thought. Ashley and Dylan had been using his bat to pound nails. That bat used to have a lot of memories. Now it just had a lot of holes.

Matt shook his head at the pitiful sight as he strolled into the batter's box. He rapped the bat on the far corner of home plate and grimaced as a couple of splinters rubbed against his palm. His bat was falling to pieces. His season was falling to pieces. Thinking about leaving was bad, but thinking about staying was worse. If only he could wait out the next two months right here in the batter's box, looking for Ty's next pitch. Matt lifted his bat. Good thing he was playing baseball up there. Good thing. Because without it . . .

He looked toward the back door, opened just a crack.

"You gonna play or what?" Matt yelled. The door flew open. Ashley and Dylan raced out to the field shouting, "We'll shag 'em! We'll shag 'em!" Axle and his tennis ball charged after them.

Matt watched them go. "Oh, man, Ross. You remember shagging for Tom?" he murmured. "When we were little kids?"

"Yeah. We used to throw his best hits back into the woods sometimes," said Ross. He squatted behind home plate, rubbed some dirt into his hands, and pushed an imaginary mask down. "Drove him insane."

Matt rocked the bat over his right shoulder. "Tom was a pushover. Fortunately, I got these guys better trained."

Ross smirked. "Yeah, you got 'em whipped. Dylan must hate your guts bad, the way he follows you around all the time." Matt put a foot on Ross's shoulder and pushed him sideways into the grass.

"Throw, Ty," called Matt. "I'm ready even if Ross ain't."

Tyler sent them in hard and a little low. Matt flipped the first couple of golf balls with a one-handed swing into the infield.

"Aw, Matt, you can hit harder'n that," complained Dylan. "Axle just swallowed that last one."

Matt felt his shoulders loosen. He listened to the pull–crouch of his stance, the mad lightning swing flickering distantly through his brain. One last swing and a miss, for humility, for luck. Then Matt let fly and started knocking them back straight into the woods.

"Yaaaaaay," screeched Ashley as she jumped into the underbrush after a tennis ball. "It's baseball!"

The Bainter Family Automatic Fielding Machine turned over for the new season as Ashley and Dylan heaved the balls infield. Axle pounced and ran them the rest of the way onto Tyler's foot. Another round of hits, and Matt's swing turned explosive. The soccer ball had just cleared third base. "The longest blooper of the evening, folks," crowed Ashley in her fake announcer's voice, when the back door opened, and Tom walked over to second base.

Matt wiped the sweat out of his eyes. He hardly dared to believe it, but here was Tom, outside, horsing around. Just like before. This was better than great. Maybe things *would* go okay. Maybe. Matt took a deep breath.

"Bad dog! Git over here!" yelled Dylan, tackling Axle before he had a chance to race infield to Tom. "You think you'd get it by now, you dumb mutt." He and

Ashley dragged the struggling dog into his kennel and chained the door shut. Axle howled with yearning, then shut up and flopped down for a nap.

"Anybody sick?" Matt raised his voice to Tyler. "Got colds or something?"

"Aw, quit your worrying," called Tom. "The only sick one is me."

"Man, he looks skinny," said Ross quietly, crouching behind the plate.

Matt blinked in surprise. "You're kidding, right? Tom looks great, up two and a half pounds since he got out of the hospital last month."

He raised the bat. "So, you out here to catch or criticize my brother?" He popped the next pitch gently to Tom—and he caught it. Tom grinned at Matt, pleased and a little surprised at the catch. Matt grinned back.

"Hit another," called Tom. Matt pushed a softball out to him and Tom caught that one, too. Matt's heart swelled with joy. He watched Tom underhand the ball to Tyler. Then he walked off the field, panting a little, and sat down on the tree stump next to the sandbox.

"See?" murmured Matt to Ross. "See there? He caught two balls. He looks good, real strong. Up two and a half pounds."

"Okay. Sure, Matt," said Ross. It sounded maybe like a question, but Matt wasn't listening anymore.

"Dylan, come in and hit," Matt yelled. He dropped the bat on the plate and strolled over to Tom. He sat down on the edge of the sandbox.

"Man, I'm starved," he said. "You hungry? 'Cause I could go in and make some sandwiches."

"Nah. You put on too much mayonnaise."

"Well, how 'bout some cookies? Kelsey baked this morning and—"

Tom smiled faintly at him. "Give it a rest, Mommy."

"You're skinny," grumbled Matt. "You shouldn't be so small. You got to be strong, going into this thing."

Tom snorted. "You packed yet?"

"Nah. I'll pack tomorrow after church. Is Marianne driving you?"

Tom nodded. "Mom's all hacked about my girlfriend going with me to check in to the hospital, but too bad. It's just preliminary blood work and enzyme counts. The big stuff starts next week."

The kitchen window flew open. Kelsey stuck out her head. "Suppertime!" she yelled. She turned to Ross and Tyler. "Mom said you guys can stay for supper if you aren't sick."

"Jeez, we ain't sick!" Ross yelled back. "You think we'd come over if we was sick?"

"Okay! Ashley, show 'em where the antiseptic wipes are. Wash up good!" The window slammed shut.

"No, me! Me! I get to show 'em what to do!" yelled

Dylan. He and Ashley galloped infield and pulled Ross and Ty into the house.

Matt glanced at Tom's face, at the bitter lines around his brother's mouth. "Kelsey's such a drag with that box of wipes," Matt said. "She's been wiping down the door handles twice a day."

"Mom gave her the list of hospital protocols," said Tom absently. "They're worried that with little kids in the house I might catch a cold, or pinkeye, or something." Matt watched him glance down at his bony fingers.

"Listen, you can borrow any of my stuff. If you want to."

The last thing Matt wanted to do was show up at a strange middle school on Monday wearing jeans and one of Tom's outer-space T-shirts, especially since Tom was going to wear nothing but hospital sweats and an IV bag for the next two months. It hurt to think about it, but all he said was "Cool. Thanks."

"Least I can do," said Tom. "Dragging you away from the baseball team."

Matt looked down as he dug his heel into the sandy grass. "Nah, it's great. Everything's great. Upper West Bexley's got a pretty good ball team."

He watched his other heel dig into the sand. "Besides, it's either me or Kelsey going, and there is no way I'm getting stuck here taking care of the little kids."

Weird. His voice started to shake. Every time the subject came up, every time his mom or dad asked him what he wanted to do, stay here or be with Tom, his voice started to shake. How could they ask him that? Didn't they know?

He realized that no, actually, they didn't. He and Tom shared a bedroom, and there was a whole winter's worth of stuff that they were both keeping quiet about—Tom's night sweats, and insomnia, and leg cramps, and those shuddering, crawling drug dreams at three in the morning. Dreams so vivid that Matt had started dreaming them, too.

He swallowed hard. Okay, so it wasn't like they were going to let him check into the hospital bed next to Tom's, but still. No way. No way was he going to be left behind. He had to back Tom up. Make sure Tom did great. That was his part of the deal.

"You sure?" asked Tom.

"Sure I'm sure. Everything's great," said Matt.

"Man, I knew you'd say that," Tom said, looking toward the woods. "You've been saying that a lot lately."

Matt felt something roll over in his chest. He studied Tom's profile, memorizing it as the kitchen window opened again, a square of yellow light shining in the falling darkness.

"You guys!" yelled Kelsey. "Mom says to haul your butts in here for supper!"

laundry basket crammed with ba

better grip, put a knee under

forward to punch another

the front door. A bunch

the penlight.

Matt's shoulder

cases weighed

were being

rate. Fi

the

**THE** next e

a sheet of p

plastic laun

paper was

numbers, and a long list of security codes. Standing next
to Matt in the rainy darkness on the Harrisons' front
steps, she squinted at the tiny print.

Matt shifted impatiently. The two extremely heavy
suitcases he carried knocked into his shins. He felt like
dropping them. The Harrisons' granite stairs were so
slick with rain, the suitcases would slide straight down
to the graveled drive and into that big puddle. That'd be
cool to watch, except then his mom would get mad, and
he had promised his dad to take it easy on her while
they were up here.

"Sixth, sixth, sevthen, oh, pound," his mom muttered
around the penlight clamped between her teeth. "No,
waid a minute—that's the back door." She nudged the

hroom stuff into a
o steady it, and leaned
de into the security box at
of swearing lisped out around

s went numb. Fortunately, the suit-
the same—two tons each—so his arms
stretched out of joint at exactly the same
e minutes more and his knuckles would brush
ground. What a great fly-ball reach he'd have then,
e thought.

"Aha!" said his mom. "Sixth, sixth, sevthen, oh, star!"
And the front door swung open.

The penlight in her mouth sagged. "Jethus God," she
whispered. They peered into the huge entry hall.

Matt felt dizzy. A weird coincidence. His mom had
whispered the same thing as she stood next to him in a
different doorway. The rainy night air of Upper West
Bexley suddenly smelled like a damp shower curtain
and Kelsey's coconut shampoo. His mom standing in
the bathroom doorway. The day he'd brought the last
can of ginger ale to Tom, sick with what looked like
the flu.

*"C'mon, Tom. Up and at 'em." He had yanked impatiently
at Tom's blankets. "We're gonna miss the first pitch."*

*Tom just lay in bed and groaned.*

*"Jeez, Tom! Cleveland's in the Series! Like I'm gonna let you miss that! We'll kick Kelsey off the couch so you can lay down. C'mon. You can't be that sick. Nobody is that sick."*

*"Go 'way." Tom's voice, muffled by the pillow.*

Matt wrestled the suitcases across the cold, dark foyer into an even colder, darker great room. "Ginger ale," he murmured.

His mom spit out the penlight. "You say something?"

*"I'm bringing you some ginger ale," he had said, giving Tom's blanket a final yank. "And then I'm hauling you into the living room."*

*Matt dashed down the hallway, leaped over Ashley's bike, around a stack of towels, through Dylan and his Lego guys strewn in front of the closet, skidded past the living room—*

*"Tom's coming to watch, so get off the couch, Kelse," he had yelled over the blare of the TV. He caught sight of the pitcher's windup. "First pitch already? Crap!"*

*—into the kitchen. Mom yakking on the phone. Fridge, last can of Mr. K's ginger ale. Past the living room with a lightning, loving glance at the batter's swing-and-a-miss. Jump through the hallway into the dim bedroom. Tom's bed empty, the sheets in a tangle on the floor.*

*"Faker," he had muttered as he sprinted through the hall.*

*He slid into the living room, his gaze glued to the TV, not willing to miss another pitch. Prime floor position, right in front of the coffee table.*

*"Like I'm gonna share with you now," he said over his shoulder to the couch. He popped the top with great satisfaction. "And this is the last can."*

*"Can I have a sip, Matt?" asked Dylan.*

*"If you rinse your mouth and leave stuff in my pop," he said, his mind on the game, "I'm gonna hurt you."*

*"Is it that cheap stuff Mom bought on sale?" Kelsey had asked from behind him, still on the couch. "I hate that stuff. I thought you said Tom was coming."*

Matt set down the suitcases and flexed his aching fingers. He looked up at the oak-beamed ceiling rising twenty-five feet above his head, the point of the arch lost in the shadowy dark.

*"I can't believe it," he muttered. "He won't even drag himself in here. He deserves to miss this." He almost hadn't gone looking for him. Almost. But something made him tear himself away from the TV.*

*"TOM!" Tom wasn't in the living room. He wasn't in the bedroom, either. He wasn't outside or in the basement. Matt found him finally, on the floor in the bathroom.*

*"Mom! MOM! Quick!"*

*"Jesus God," whispered his mom, standing in the doorway.*

*She turned. "Get him in the car, Matt." She ran down the hallway, grabbing her keys off the hook by the door. "Kelsey! Call your dad and tell him we're at the clinic!"*

His mom set the laundry basket on top of the suitcases. "Stay here, honey. Let me find a light switch." She disappeared into the gloom. Her voice echoed off to the left. "Do rich people even use light switches? Because I am not looking up another code on that—"

She must have crossed a motion detector. The hall suddenly flooded with amber light—all of it shining through an enormous, backlit stained-glass window of Saint George and the dragon. Colored glass covered the entire far wall. Matt and his mom stared at the castle, the rearing charger, the sword in Saint George's hand, the mischievous look on the dragon's face.

*"Go to the hospital," said the clinic doctor. "By the time we get the ambulance called, you could have him there. I'll meet you in Emergency."*

*"Matt? Did I bring his insurance card?" his mom asked faintly. "I don't think I brought his card."*

*"We'll worry about that part later, Mrs. Bainter," the doctor said. "Just get him there."*

"I'm speechless," said his mom, staring at the stained glass. "You ever seen something to beat that?"

Matt shook his head. "Nope. Never seen anything like it."

*"Yeah, I've seen plenty like it," said the oncologist, two days after that crazy, careening car ride. He sat on a folding chair in Tom's hospital room. "Too many. Bone scan, biopsy surgery"—he flipped through the medical chart and sighed—"worst-case diagnosis. You've got bone cancer. The tumor we removed from your left hipbone was malignant, Tom. I'm sorry." He looked at them all—Matt, his family—gathered around Tom's bed. "I'm very sorry."*

Matt blinked at the dragon. By the time Tom had started outpatient chemotherapy and then radiation ten days after his surgery, the World Series was over. Cleveland in the Series. And Matt had missed the show.

Except for that one swing-and-a-miss.

*"Every time your doctor puts you back in here, you end up being the biggest train wreck on my floor, kiddo," one of the nurses had said, taking Tom's pulse. "You've had every severe immune reaction, every secondary infection, every radiation burn I can think of."*

*"He studied the list in the cancer patient's handbook," said Matt, lounging in the visitor's chair, keeping Tom company. "He thought he'd try 'em all."*

*"Shut up," whispered Tom, his eyes closed.*

**20**

The nurse snorted. "I can believe that. The oncologists have stopped chemo, started chemo, switched drugs, switched drugs some more." She made a note on his chart. "These enzyme reports on your liver make me want to cry."

"He's fighting it, though," said Matt. "He's tough."

"Tough," whispered Tom.

"Yeah, well, in case nobody's told you, Tom, the object is to stop messing around here with your primary treatments," said the nurse. "It's time we kick you out for good. They're waiting for you in Columbus."

The laundry basket slid off the top of the suitcases and crashed to the Oriental carpet. Rolls of toilet paper, bars of soap flew everywhere. Matt's mom shrieked and lunged for the conditioner.

"Whew! I about had a heart attack," she said, turning the screw top firmly. "I don't know how to spot clean imported carpets." She loaded up the basket. "C'mon. Let's get this stuff upstairs before we wreck something."

They lugged everything up the curving marble staircase.

"Lessee," said his mom, consulting the Harrisons' house-sitting instructions again, "you're in Rickey Harrison's room. I'm down the hall in the master suite." She looked up. "Page me on the intercom when you're unpacked, and we'll scout out the kitchen."

About the only cleaning Rickey Harrison had managed to do before taking off with the folks for Africa was to clear out one bureau drawer and the top of the desk. Matt jammed his socks and underwear in the drawer. He found some room in the front of the bedroom closet stuffed with the hockey sticks and Game Boys and winter clothes of a total stranger. The whole house was like that. Eighteen silent rooms crammed with furniture, closets bulging with guest towels and leather coats and lacrosse equipment. He and his mom wandered all over looking for a place to store their empty suitcases. They took them down to the garage, finally, and locked them in the trunk of the car.

"Well," said his mom, slamming the trunk shut. "Quite the loaner home, huh? Close to the hospital and all. Nice of Doc Harrison to let us house-sit while they're on that mission trip."

"Yep," said Matt. "I've never seen a chandelier in a garage before."

Matt's mom looked up, considering. "That's not a chandelier. Not exactly." She ran her fingers through her hair. "I'm beat. I don't have the energy to find the Florida room where I can smoke, and I need a cigarette bad." She opened the car door and slid behind the wheel. Matt got in the passenger side.

She leaned against the headrest and blew out a stream of smoke. "You nervous about tomorrow?"

"Nah." Matt cracked open the car window. "Upper

West got beat in sectionals last year because of a weak outfield. Coach Pangbourn can't wait for me to transfer. Everything's great." He stared through the windshield at the closed garage door, proud of his steady voice. His mom would never guess how shaky he really felt.

"Good. I told Tom I'd try to get there before doctors' rounds in the morning." She flipped open the ashtray. "It's just blood work and enzymes. The treatment starts next week. So. You okay with getting on the school bus by yourself?"

Matt snorted. "I'm thirteen, Mom, not three."

She grinned tiredly. "Right. I keep forgetting. Okay, Mr. Maturity, we'll meet back here tomorrow for supper. I'll cook chicken. You can tell me about school, and I can tell you about Tom."

To be honest, though, Matt *was* a little nervous about tomorrow. New school. Find the right classrooms. Meet the teachers. Everybody a stranger. It'd be weird not having Ross and Tyler to horse around with. So, after climbing between the sheets on Rickey Harrison's king-sized bed, after lying there in the dark, staring up at the ceiling, thinking—about school . . . about Tom . . . about baseball—Matt's thoughts naturally drifted toward home. He thought about the day Tom had helped him figure out baseball.

How old had he been? Six, seven years old, maybe. Ross and Ty had come over, and the three of them had watched Tom pull Ashley's old crib mattress out of the junk pile meant for the landfill. He tied it to the trunk of the pine tree. Then he drew a circle target on cardboard and taped it to the mattress. He looked them over as they took turns throwing at the target.

When Tyler hit the bull's-eye nine out of ten, Tom said, "Well. I sure can't teach you a thing about aim. But you got to get up some speed, otherwise the batter is going to knock you on your butt every time."

He pushed Ross into a squat in front of the mattress, taped the cardboard target square on Ross's T-shirt, stuck his own big glove on Ross's little hand. "There ya go, Ty. Throw it until Ross says ouch."

After a couple of *ouch*es, Tom said, "Come here and hit, Matt. Stand like this. Nah, crouch down more and hold your elbows away from your body. Keep your wrists straight. Take the bat off your shoulder." Tom poked and prodded at Matt until he was satisfied. A perfect textbook batting stance.

He squatted down and looked Matt straight in the eye. "I bet you fifty bucks you can't hit the ball past second base." Matt had stuck out his jaw.

Matt rolled over onto his side in Rickey Harrison's bed and grinned. Fifty bucks. Tom was always betting him fifty bucks. Fifty bucks Matt couldn't finish his spelling sheet before bedtime. Fifty bucks he couldn't carry the biggest bag of groceries in the house *and* put it all away. Fifty bucks he couldn't let Mom wash his hair to get the bicycle grease out without screaming down the house. And, man, he fell for it every time. Over and over.

That time in the backyard was no different. "Fifty bucks," repeated Tom.

Matt had stuck an elbow in Tom's stomach and pushed him away. "Get outta my way and let me *hit*."

"Atta boy, Matt," said Tom, standing up. He punched Matt on the shoulder, messing up his perfect stance. "Go get 'em."

It took Matt the rest of the spring to figure out how to get some power out of that stance. But once he started to hit Tyler's pitches, once Ross stopped saying "Ouch," the three of them tore up the Little League brackets. Tore up the school leagues. And they sure weren't finished yet.

Matt felt warm and a little sleepy. He rubbed his eyes. Tom never really played much organized ball after that. A couple of months later he went to seventh grade, where he started reading science fiction and hanging around with Marianne Philpots instead. Like he'd figured out that his own place in baseball was on the top row of the bleachers, watching his amazing little brother belt them all over the park. But there was no denying that Tom had given him the gift. The gift that drove his life as surely as the very beating of his heart. It was Tom who had given him baseball.

And so, for the thousandth time, Matt thought that the least he could do for Tom was get him through this one last treatment. And when Tom came home in one piece, finally, Matt could relax. Get on with the rest of his life. That was the deal. Pure simple.

Matt closed his eyes. He covered up good in Rickey Harrison's blanket, right up to his ears. He yawned once—a huge, slow yawn. Tom's voice murmured him to sleep: *"Atta boy, Matt. Go get 'em."*

## GREAT MOMENTS IN
## COLLEGE BASEBALL

**UPPER** West Bexley Middle School was the classiest school building Matt had ever seen. From the outside it looked like the new administration wing of the county hospital—all smoked-glass windows filled with fern baskets and exposed brick walls set in soothing patterns that drew your eye upward and made you meditate on the importance of good health and higher education. Three gated tennis courts and the school's white-domed observatory stood next to the south wing of the school. And though he couldn't see it from the front entrance where he stood, Matt knew exactly where Upper West's ball diamond was. Just down that grassy slope, the base paths raked smooth as glass, chalk lines glinting in the sun.

Matt walked through the door, a serene and cocky look hiding his pounding heart. He came to a halt under the rotunda. A hundred million strange kids milled around, everybody talking but him. Matt's stomach lurched. This was going to be hard. Fortunately, before it got too hard, Matt spied Coach Pangbourn standing near the trophy case. She was looking over the crowd, waiting for him.

Matt walked over. "Hey, Coach, how's it going?"

"All right, Matt. Very all right, now that you're here." She shook his hand. "Welcome to Upper West."

Matt shook back. She sure was dressed up for a coach, wearing a bright red business suit and dangly gold earrings. Maybe a rich school like Upper West had a strict dress code for its gym teachers. "So, Coach. Can you point me toward the Head Guy's office?"

Coach raised an eyebrow. "Excuse me?"

"The principal. I got to find him and get transferred."

Coach Pangbourn raised the other eyebrow in surprise, but all she said was, "Sure, Matt. The office is right down this hallway." She opened a door and led Matt into a standard-issue, middle-school principal's office.

"Have a seat, Matt. I'll be right back."

Matt opened his mouth to tell her she didn't have to hang around and introduce him to the principal, but Coach Pangbourn was out the door.

A bell rang. Matt took the seat beside the desk. His gaze fell on the greatest photograph ever to hold down a stack of papers on a principal's desk—a big framed picture of Ohio State's "Lightning Strikes Twice" Division I Women's Softball Champs (1989–1991). And there was Lisa Lewis way back then, looking young and kind of cute, smack in the middle of the team holding up the 1991 trophy with those long arms of hers.

Matt frowned. Weird, Upper West's principal having that particular photo on his desk. Maybe Lisa was his cousin or something. Matt took another quick look, just to be sure. Yep, that was her, all right, the same photo in the girl chapter they had tossed into the back of *Great Moments in College Baseball*. He had worn out that book, borrowing it from the Amesville public library. So Matt knew her right away. There was no mistaking Lisa Lewis, Ohio State's two-time MVP, All-American shortstop. Her national records for double plays and throw-outs at home still stood after more than ten years. Too bad she was a girl and everything and had to dink around playing softball. With all that talent, she could have turned pro.

Another bell rang. The principal still hadn't showed. Matt got up and prowled around the room, stopping at the window. If he plastered the right side of his face against the glass, he could just see Upper West's ball diamond off to the left. A janitor was on a riding mower, making neat diagonal lines back and forth across the infield. March 21. First cut of the season. Even at Amesville Middle School, back on that pit of a ball field where the grass turned brown in May and the base paths were packed so hard that sliding into second was like body slamming concrete—even back home at Amesville right now the grass was coming up green and tender and smelling like spring. . . .

The office door banged open. Matt jumped. Coach Pangbourn came in, balancing a donut on top of a coffee mug in one hand and a thick manila folder, a class schedule book full of sticky notes, and a couple of pencils in the other. She smiled at him—and the light dawned.

"You're Lisa Lewis!"

Coach Pangbourn laughed. "Boy. Those were the days, huh?"

She sat down behind the principal's desk and offloaded the donut, the coffee mug, the schedule forms, and the manila folder with BAINTER, MATTHEW L. laserprinted across the top.

Matt collapsed into the chair next to the desk. Good grief. Instead of turning pro, Lisa Lewis had turned into Mrs. Pangbourn, principal of Upper West Bexley Middle School. Head baseball coach. Why hadn't anybody bothered to tell him?

Mrs. Pangbourn tossed the pencils into an empty cup on her desk. "Kind of a shock, huh? Relax, Matt. Being a principal is just what I do to make a living. Baseball, on the other hand . . ." She looked him over. "You're wearing the tie for me?"

Matt hunched his shoulders, embarrassed. "Yeah. Well, not exactly for you. I mean, I thought I'd impress the baseball coach with my manners and all, because lady coaches like that kind of stuff. See, I didn't know you were . . ."

"Also the principal?"

Matt nodded.

Mrs. Pangbourn sipped her coffee. "Speaking as Upper West's lady baseball coach, I must say I'm impressed every year when the ball teams from Amesville run up here to beat us three for three."

She pulled the folder toward her. "Now, I know you played as a sixth-grader on Amesville's seventh-grade team last year. Along with the catcher—what's his name?"

"Ross Berg."

"Uh-huh. And Tyler Smith. I made sure to find out your pitcher's name after he threw that shutout in game two. And as for your bat—" Mrs. Pangbourn shook her head reproachfully. "You really knocked the heck out of Jason Thornberg's change-up. The ball kept missing his head by an inch. Poor kid's been shaking like a leaf ever since."

Matt shrugged modestly.

"Okaaay. Since you're transferring at the beginning of the season, let's not beat around the bush. You'll go through tryouts, play center field for Upper West.

We're definitely moving you up to the eighth-grade team. Third bat. We'll be in the playoffs before you know it. I'm looking forward to coaching you, Matt. By the end of May, when you go back to Amesville, we'll have that little problem with your right wrist straightened out."

Matt glanced down at his right wrist sticking out of the cuff of his white shirt. It looked okay to him.

"'Course, baseball's not all we do around here. We aim to be a full-service school, so speaking as the lady principal, let's take a peek at your academic record." Mrs. Pangbourn opened the manila folder. She flipped through a couple of pages. "Uh-oh."

"Bad, huh?"

"Hmm. Let's just say I'm underwhelmed. Your record's pretty erratic. Take these standardized test scores. Out of a possible five hundred in science, you scored four hundred ninety-seven, which has to be one of the top scores in the state. On the other hand, you got a pitiful one hundred fifty-two on the writing section."

She glanced up. "You're not the family genius, are you? Because if you are, we gotta do something about your communication skills. Scores like this"—she tapped the papers—"make people think you're operating with the brains of a squid."

Matt blinked in surprise. Genius? Did every family have a genius?

Because he was pretty sure his family didn't. Tom was the open-hearted, funny Bainter, the one every teacher secretly liked the best. Kelsey was the joiner. Only a sophomore in high school, but she was on every advisory board, in every school club, at every pep rally. Definitely the Bainter most likely to succeed.

And the little kids, the ones charging up like a weird echo of the older kids: Ashley, almost nine years old and following straight in Kelsey's organized footsteps. And Dylan was such a funny little kid. Every morning he had to kick Dylan's butt off the bus at the first-grade stop; otherwise, Dylan hid underneath a seat, trying to ride all the way to middle school with Matt. Same thing Matt had tried all those years ago, ducking under the seat, trying to ride all the way with Tom. . . . Tom . . .

Matt blinked again. Two ahead of him, two behind. For the first time in his life, he realized what that made him. The Bainter holding down the center. The one who played up with the semipro teens and down with the rank amateur kids. So that's where his huge center-field talent came from. He'd been born into it. The thought made him grin.

But all he said was, "A squid? No way. I talk way more than any squid."

Mrs. Pangbourn snorted. "You gotta do better than this, Matt," she said, pulling a seventh-grade class schedule toward her. "There's the little matter of eligibility. Which I decide, by the way. You pull a C average in Mrs. Tinker's English-with-training-wheels class, or you are off the ball team."

She was quiet a moment, writing. "I'd like to meet your mom sometime."

Matt's gaze wandered around her office. "She's with my older brother, Tom. He's in the hospital. He's got to have this thing done."

Matt frowned, thinking. Tom had looked tired and slow yesterday, climbing into Marianne's car. He looked thin. He should be bigger, stronger. Matt wished he had nagged Tom more about drinking soy protein shakes and working out with the two-pound weights Matt had swiped from the high school weight room, but they plain ran out of time. The oncologist said, "We do it now," and bam, here they were. Doing it. Stuff happened so fast.

"I know," said Mrs. Pangbourn, closing the manila folder and looking at him. "When Amesville sent me your records, your principal told me about Tom. About you and your mom up here. The rest of your family back home. I'm sorry. This must be hard."

What was hard was having to do all the talking. No Ashley and Dylan interrupting with a million stupid questions about what a squid eats. No Kelsey barging in with a plateful of brownies, wondering if she could catch a ride with Mrs. Pangbourn back into town.

And no Tom, either. Nothing but the quiet sympathy in Mrs. Pangbourn's eyes. Matt cleared his throat. He tried to figure out how Kelsey would handle it.

"Oh, no, it's great. This bone marrow transplant works great. They already got some of Tom's marrow cells purged of the cancer and stuff. Now all they got to do is totally destroy his diseased bone marrow with a couple of drugs, stick the harvested cells back in, we go home, and Tom's all set. The last treatment, and then he's done."

"Uh, Matt?"

"Yeah?"

"You've got your eyes closed, talking to me."

Matt opened his eyes and grinned, saying again what he always said these days. "It's great, Coach Pangbourn. Everything's going to work out great."

And it was great. Everything was great. Strange and different and lonely, but great. Matt took off his tie and rolled up his sleeves. Walking alone into first period was weird. Then he sat through English and math and got lost in the hallways trying to find room 307—Introduction to Art. Art turned out to be pretty interesting. He and a couple of guys horsed around, making a huge, snakey turd out of clay. Then the three of them went through the lunch line together, making gross noises as the cafeteria ladies rolled their eyes and ladled out excellent food that no way came out of a food-service can—

linguine, mixed vegetables, and a fresh pear so golden and ripe it looked fake.

"So. You guys play baseball?" asked Matt.

The guys from art class introduced him around a little bit, then walked him over to the science lab. The advanced biology class had just come back from a field trip to the Bahamas during spring break. A trip to the Bahamas. Whoa, thought Matt. Way cooler than touring the boot factory in Nelsonville, which is where *his* sixth-grade class had gone last year. Matt shook his head in wonder.

Everybody was still picking the sand out of their hair and comparing tans, so Dr. Evers didn't make them do much. By that time, the seventh-grade girls had gotten a good look at the new boy from Amesville, and they twittered around him until the dismissal bell rang. Matt did what he always did when the girls gathered around—he relaxed and enjoyed it.

Mrs. Pangbourn stopped him in the hallway. "So how'd it go?"

Matt shifted his book bag to the other shoulder. "Pretty okay. Nobody spit on me or anything."

Mrs. Pangbourn laughed. "Most of these kids have gone to school together since kindergarten. Believe me, they are sick and tired of each other."

"Hiya, Matt," said a girl as she breezed by him in the hall. Her three friends broke into squealing giggles.

"Bye-yah, Matt," said the girl. The squealing got louder.

Mrs. Pangbourn raised an eyebrow. "You seem to be a welcome diversion around here."

"Hey, Matt, which bus you riding?" One of the snake guys from art slapped his backpack. "Because I can show you where." The guy looked up. "That okay, Mrs. P?"

"Absolutely," said Mrs. Pangbourn. "But you better hustle."

The bus dropped him off at the foot of the Harrisons' graveled drive. A couple of girls waved and yelled, "Bye-yah, Matt!" out the windows. Everybody else ignored him. Nobody spit. Matt was relieved.

He walked the winding driveway past a tall stand of hundred-year-old oaks. He glanced at the stone towers and iron balconies looming three stories over his head as he punched in the door code. He tossed his backpack on the butcher block, washed his hands, and nuked a burrito in the microwave. He ate it over the sink, popped a few cookies in his mouth, and dragged his backpack upstairs to Rickey Harrison's room.

He wandered idly back downstairs through the silent rooms, through the dining room, parlor; walked across the great hall and watched Saint George light up; past the living room, study, billiard room, and into the Florida room, where he found his mom.

Every window was open; every filmy curtain billowed in the chilly March wind. Matt thought his mom looked right at home, like she'd been there all afternoon, hunched over a plaid beanbag ashtray, chainsmoking. Unfortunately, she also looked mad enough to bust.

"Your brother," she said, glaring at him, the smoke puffing out of her mouth like Saint George's dragon, "checked himself out of the hospital this morning. Before I got there. He went off and got married. Nineteen years old, sick as a dog, and *married*. Jesus God."

## UP FROM THE MINORS

**WHICH** made Marianne Philpots Matt's brand-new sister-in-law.

Matt figured they must have spent the night at a Holiday Inn or something, because Tom and Marianne didn't show up at the Harrisons' house until Tuesday. Matt rode the sports bus home after tryouts and found his mom and the honeymooners sitting tight-lipped and silent in the Florida room.

"Whoa," said Matt, edging out of the room. "I'll come back later."

"No way," said Tom. He grabbed Marianne's hand and stood up. "We were just leaving."

"Congratulations, by the way," called Matt as they retreated toward the stairs. "You, too, Marianne."

"Bet you fifty bucks I am the happiest guy on the planet," came Tom's voice from halfway up the stairs. Matt grinned.

His mom crossed her arms. "I put them in the guest

room," she said caustically. "The one with the hot tub in the bathroom."

"Good thinking, Mom," Matt said, feeling a little jealous. Rickey Harrison's bathroom just had a regular shower, nothing fancy. "So does that mean you're not totally hacked?"

His mom snorted. "When I told your dad on the phone last night, he made me swear not to start anything until he comes up Friday." She fired up another cigarette and inhaled furiously. "So I'm not. Starting anything." She stuck the cigarette in the corner of her mouth, crossed her arms, and glared at Matt. Daring him to start something.

Matt held up his hands in peace. She threw a pillow at him anyway.

In a house that big, not starting anything turned out to be easy. They had a polite breakfast together Wednesday and Thursday mornings. For the rest of the day they stayed out of each other's hair. His mom made herself scarce. Tom and Marianne spent a whole lot of time upstairs in the guest room. Matt went to school and stayed late for tryouts. That was about it.

Except Thursday evening, Matt (halfway up the stairs) bumped into Marianne (halfway down the stairs), a tray in her hands. The dishes clattered and slipped.

"Whoa, careful," she said. She stopped on the step right above his. "How's it going?"

Matt looked up at her, considering. Marianne was a lousy hitter but pretty sharp with a glove, so Matt usually picked her third for his team during those endless pickup games in the backyard over the years. Put her in left field, mostly. Left field in the backyard, left field at church softball games, left field all summer long after the last Little League game of the night; and the players and spectators horsed around playing slug ball until way past ten o'clock. Marianne played left. He played center. Not surprising they had developed an easy rhythm of shift and cover, backup and glove work.

The thing was, he knew Marianne pretty well. So when she said, "How's it going?" he knew she wasn't asking about school or ball practice or homework. She was asking about the big stuff. The important stuff.

"You're screwed, Marianne," he said. "Mom is totally chopped."

"Shoot." She thumped down on the step. He sat down next to her, the tray at their feet. A couple of gingersnaps on a plate. Matt sniffed approvingly at the familiar stink of vanilla soy drink drifting from the empty glass.

She bit her lip. "I guess if my mom was alive, she'd be mad, too. My dad's sure not very happy with me." She looked up. "But I am. Happy, I mean." She blushed.

"So's Tom," said Matt. "I heard him whistling 'Here Comes the Bride' to Saint George last night."

"You happy, Matt?" asked Marianne softly.

He rotated his shoulders, trying to loosen them up. Marianne was okay, but Tom needed to get going on his preliminary blood work and enzymes. He needed to concentrate on the big stuff that came after that. Married? What kind of pointless, insane thing was that to do? It was almost like . . .Tom wasn't working on getting better anymore. And screw *that,* not doing everything right. That was what they were here for. They had to do everything *right.* Matt clenched his jaw.

But Marianne just stared at him with her big, sad eyes. And he knew he couldn't bust her for this stupid marriage thing. Besides, rage would only take his head out of the game. He had to stay focused.

"It's great, Marianne." Matt dug his toe into the carpet on the stair. "Just great." He paused, struck by a thought. "Hey. I should go home. You stay here with him." Weird, how happy that made him feel, passing off the hospital watch.

Marianne blinked. "You're kidding, right? I'm no good at being tough for him. The way you and your mom are. And he needs tough right now."

*Tough.* He blew out his breath, resigned. Everybody needed tough out of him. Okay, tough it was. He pushed her shoulder, a friendly sister-in-law left-field shove. "Aw, c'mon, Marianne. You're tough. You got hit by a lot of pitches. I never saw you cry once."

Marianne shook her head. "This is different," she said, picking up the tray with trembling hands and starting down the stairs. "This is way different."

Matt leaned back. He tried to make out the ceiling somewhere at the top of all those shadows. What a cave they were living in. "Okay, Marianne," he said to the ceiling. "Anyway, if you hang around here, Mom would probably end up strangling you."

Marianne stopped at the bottom of the stairs and looked up at him. "Way deep down inside, she likes me. I think."

Friday morning, his mom skipped breakfast, and the three of them—Tom, Marianne, and Matt—kept shooting glances up the stairs, wondering when she was going to blow. When Matt got home from school, his mom was muttering under her breath. A terrible sign. Frankly, his dad drove the van up the Harrisons' circular drive not a moment too soon.

Matt's dad hugged Matt and Matt's mom. Then he unloaded box after box marked *Wedding Decor* in Kelsey's loopy handwriting.

"We brought a party," said Ashley. She hugged Marianne around the hips. "'Cause you got married."

Matt's mom muttered something under her breath. His dad shot Matt a questioning glance. Matt shrugged.

"I'm pretending I didn't hear that, Beth," said Matt's

dad, steering her away from the group around the van.

"Everybody's pretending they didn't hear that, Dad," yelled Tom. Marianne buried her face in her hands and moaned. Matt choked back a laugh.

Saturday after lunch, Kelsey and Ashley hauled all the *Wedding Decor* boxes into the dining room. Matt played Wiffle ball on the tennis court with Dylan while Tom and Marianne took another shot at married life in the guest room. Matt's mom and dad took off in the van to do errands, or to look around, or to get things straightened out, maybe. A trip that Matt realized did not go too well. By the time they all sat down to supper, his mom was in a poisonous mood.

"Columbus," she snapped, "is not my favorite place." She pushed away her spaghetti, uneaten. The plate knocked into the huge centerpiece built up in the middle of the table. A crepe-paper wedding bell tipped onto the plate and soaked up meat sauce. Matt glanced toward Tom and Marianne, down at the other end of the table.

"And Upper West Bexley," continued Matt's mom. "Nice of Doc Harrison to lend his house and all, but Upper West Bexley, Jesus God. Like camping out in the richest suburb of hell."

"Beth," said Matt's dad quietly.

Tom peered around Ashley's Barbie and Ken dolls dressed up in a bridal gown and tuxedo. "Hey, Kelse?

You over there? I want some of that cake."

"Cake, cake," chanted Dylan happily. He tugged on Matt's shirt. "It's chocolate," he confided. "Kelsey let me lick the bowl."

"Presents first," said Kelsey. She set a white-wrapped box in front of Tom and Marianne. "Congratulations, you guys."

"Whoa," said Tom. "A present. Excellent."

"You shouldn't have gotten a present and everything," said Marianne softly. She flicked a glance at Matt's mom. "I know you hadn't exactly planned on this."

The present was a yellow Crock-Pot. Matt wondered what exactly a Crock-Pot did.

"Now if it's the wrong color for your kitchen," said Kelsey anxiously, "they have 'em in blue and green so it'd be real easy to exchange—"

Matt watched the expression on his mother's face. After going four days without starting anything, he knew she wasn't about to put up with this one minute more. Sure enough.

"I am not going to put up with this one minute more," she said, glaring past the acre of tablecloth and festive wedding bells, past smiling Barbie and Ken and the messy rows of milk glasses and smeary paper napkins, straight at the happy couple. "Let me get right to the point. You are two idiots."

"Mom. Please," said Tom.

"You both put your foot in it. Divorce is totally out of the question. You can't split up when one of you is a week away from a serious-risk medical procedure. And as far as an annulment—forget it. Not after what went on upstairs this week."

Matt stared hard at his plate. He wouldn't, would *not* look over at Tom. If he did, they'd both start to grin, and then his mom would really fly off the handle. Tom knew as well as he did the best way to handle his mom. Give her a chance to get hacked and get over it. Above all, don't talk back—at least, not for a while.

But marriage had done weird things to Tom's brain, because he started right in defending himself and Marianne. "We got married because we love each other. It's not the end of the world."

Matt rolled his eyes at Tom as his mom exploded. "Well, maybe it *is* the end of the world! I can't understand how you think you're going to make it. Good grief, Tom, how do you think you're going to live—"

She closed her mouth and turned pale, like she had just blurted out the most perverse, obscene thing in the world. Her elbow, trembling, knocked gently into the Parmesan cheese.

*How do you think you're going to live* echoed around the silent table. Matt stared at his plate. Okay. Okay, the marriage was pointless and insane. So what? That just made it one more pointless and insane thing to deal with. And his family was expert at dealing with pointless and insane. They'd had a lot of practice since that day he and his mom had found Tom on the floor in the bathroom.

Dylan leaned over and whispered, "Is Mommy crying?"

Matt looked up, startled. He saw his mom swipe once at her eyes with her fingers. It was hard to believe. The only time he'd ever seen his mom cry was the night Grandpa died. And maybe that one time in the hospital, when Tom's oncologist mentioned the bone marrow transplant. "We're talking about the treatment of last resort," the doctor had said. Last resort, last resort. Even Matt had to admit that didn't sound so hot. It was possible his mom's eyes had sort of glittered a little before she turned away and looked out Tom's hospital window.

Dylan tugged anxiously on his shirt. "Is she crying, Matt? Matt?"

Marianne cleared her throat. "Everything's going to be fine," she said.

And frankly, Matt could feel Marianne's quiet words yank him a step back from the edge of the cliff he pretended didn't exist. *Treatment of last resort*. What that doctor meant was, this marrow transplant was Tom's last treatment. And his mom's eyes had filled with hope before she turned and looked out the window. That's how it was. Everybody knew that.

Matt leaned over to Dylan. "She's got an eyelash or something in her eye. So is the cake pure chocolate or that chocolate marble junk?"

Marianne took a breath. "Anyway, we meant it, Mrs. Bainter," she said. "What we promised each other. We meant it forever."

"Jesus God almighty," Matt's mother sighed wearily. "It's like reasoning with a couple of cans of paint. You have no idea what you're in for."

Tom didn't say anything at first. He just picked up his plate of spaghetti mess and headed toward the kitchen, his jaw a little tight. "Yep. You can say that again, Mom. We have no idea. Life is a mystery."

Dylan pinched Matt's elbow. "Chocolate chocolate," he said, totally satisfied. "Real good chocolate."

Kelsey jumped up and stacked plates. "Tom, bring in the cake, willya?" she yelled.

"Hey. This is my wedding reception. What am I doing in the kitchen working?"

"Matt, go help him," said Kelsey distractedly.

Matt went into the kitchen and found Tom staring at a gigantic, homemade devil's food wedding cake. He looked at Matt.

"How am I supposed to carry this thing?" he complained. "It must weigh thirty pounds."

Ashley's orange-and-yellow construction-paper daisy chains had bled a little around the edges into the mint-green icing. "Three levels. That's six pieces each, easy," said Matt.

"You can have five of mine," said Tom. He rummaged through the cupboards. "You know what a cake like this needs? Candles. A whole lotta candles."

Matt's dad came in, carrying a stack of greasy plates. "Kelsey wants to know what's the holdup."

"We're hanging around in here until Mom calms down," said Matt. He put a ring of blue candles around one of Ashley's paper flowers.

"Do it like that, and dessert will go up in flames before our very eyes," observed his dad. "You know your mom. She's fine now, patting Marianne's hand and welcoming her to the family."

Tom sat down on a kitchen stool and sighed. "Mom better be happy we got married," he muttered. "If she knew how much Marianne and me'd been fooling around before I got too sick, I sure wouldn't need new marrow. Because I'd be dead and Mom would be in jail for murdering her kid."

"Yeah?" said Matt, interested. "So fooling around, like you mean—"

"Just put the candles on the cake, Matt," said his dad.

"I don't want cancer to be the only thing going on in my life," said Tom softly. "I can't stand that."

Matt tried not to think about that, tried hard not to think about anything like that. He glanced uneasily at his dad. His dad was the only cop Amesville had. He never took the entire weekend off, never. Not even after Tom's biopsy surgery last year. Yet there he was, leaning on the counter looking tired and frustrated, half the weekend gone.

"Well, now you got one of the bigger somethings going on," said his dad. "A wife. Hoo boy."

"You don't think we love each other enough, do you?"

"Love," said his dad. He rubbed his face. "Now there I have no doubt. You and Marianne sure love each other, all right." Tom grinned.

Kelsey burst through the door. "What in the world is taking— Hey! Candles! Great idea, Matt!"

Shortly after midnight, Matt hit the kitchen for his fourth piece of cake. Even with seven noisy Bainters sacked out in the various bedrooms, the house maintained its cool serenity. The kitchen was dimly lit, tidy and quiet. Matt carved into the last half of the second layer. He wandered down to the recreation room in the basement, fork held cigarlike in his mouth as he went down the stairs.

He scooted between the leather couch and the sliding glass patio doors and settled in front of the TV. The stuff that happened at supper had really made him feel strange. So strange that he didn't bother changing the channel to the sports network. He ended up forking down the cake in front of a young people's concert, of all things—tubas, oboes, and a football field of violins. The musicians played something slow and mournful on a two-thousand-watt stage while the conductor sneered at somebody in the second violins and waggled his baton in the air.

Next thing, the camera cut over close to the lead-off cello. The poor guy wore the saddest expression Matt had ever seen on public television. Weird. As the guy dragged his bow across the strings, Matt could hear the wind in the pine tree outside the bedroom he shared with Tom back home. Long, soft needles. "Matt husha Matt," it had sung between the branches on the night before Tom started chemo.

*"You cold, Tom? I got an extra blanket."*

*"Nah. Just restless. Can't sleep."*

*But Matt had gotten up and laid his blanket over Tom anyway. Covered him up good, right up to his ears. "Just in case. It's pretty cold outside. A lot of wind tonight."*

*"Yeah, okay. Thanks, Matt."*

Carefully, Matt set his plate on the couch next to the remote. He leaned forward until his elbows rested on his knees. His fingers folded into each other. Here is the church. Here is the steeple. Here is the door, oh, God—

The cello guy looked up. Looked straight out of the screen, stared into Matt's eyes. Matt froze.

After a minute, Matt leaned the rest of the way over and made sure the patio doors were shut tight. Just in case. Just in case the dark, fearful air bearing down all around him turned out to be nothing more than an early spring thunderstorm on its way to drench Upper West Bexley. His elbow, trembling, knocked his crumby fork clear to the carpet.

# 5

## THE BEGINNING OF THE SEASON

**SUNDAY** evening, Matt stood on the porch and waved good-bye. He waved to Kelsey and Ashley and Dylan as his dad drove them back to Amesville and school the next morning. He waved to Marianne as she drove back to her apartment and her job as a nurse's aide at the Ten-Mile-High Nursing Home. The next morning, Matt got up and fixed Tom breakfast.

"Up and at 'em," he said to the mound of blankets in the middle of the guest-room bed. "The quicker you get this bone thing over with, the quicker we all go home."

Matt couldn't find a tray anywhere in the kitchen, so he had loaded the toast and box of cereal and a big, tall glass of soy drink onto a cookie sheet. The cereal spoon slid from one end to the other as he set the cookie sheet on the night table.

"Ugh. It's that puke soy stuff. I don't think I can face it," said Tom's voice, muffled by all the blankets.

Matt nudged the drink closer toward the lump he

thought was Tom's head. "So you can smell it all the way under there, huh?" He leaned over and prodded the blankets. "All week you drank Marianne's. And I bet she never put in extra cinnamon like I do."

Tom hauled himself to an upright position and leaned against the headboard. "You ever drink that crap?" he asked.

Matt snorted. "Do I look stupid?"

Tom looked distastefully at the cookie sheet. "Believe me, burping up chemo drugs all day long tastes way better."

Matt grinned and pulled the drapes. A little daylight entered the room.

"Man, I hate this," muttered Tom.

"What?"

"Every morning I wake up. I feel okay until I get a look at my arms," he said. He held them out. Two skinny broom handles, faded black and blue and puffy at the wrist and elbow from the last round of needle sticks. "Then I remember I'm screwed."

Matt looked out at the line of trees curving along the driveway down below. He didn't want to think about that. He wanted to think about the weight Tom had gained last week. One more precious pound, going into this thing.

"You still got hair," he blurted out to the furry-feeling curtains. "A little. That's gotta be a good sign."

He turned around. Tom, bitter lines at his mouth again, was looking him over. But all he said was, "I bet you fifty bucks you can't drink this whole glass gone."

"Gimme a break. Besides, you already owe me about ten thousand dollars."

"Hey, I am totally serious with this one. My insurance from the lumberyard capped out, so the Baptist Society is picking up the tab for the treatment up here. We'll just stick in the bill between the sterile irrigation packs and the burn creme—'Payment to brother for nutritional assistance rendered.'"

Tom looked up at the ceiling. "Because if we don't get rid of that smell like right now, I'm gonna hurl."

But Matt was tough. He nagged until Tom drank half. Then he grabbed his backpack while Tom was still moaning and whining about drinking the other half and beat it out the door just in time for the bus to school.

He came home that afternoon to an empty house. No surprise there. He knew the routine. His mom was at the hospital, hanging there pretty much round the clock for the next couple of days, holding the barf pan as Tom threw up every fifteen minutes. When she wasn't busy wiping off Tom's mouth, she'd be nagging the nurses about chart updates or talking on the pay phone in the hospital lobby, lining up huge wads of Baptist Society cash to pay the unbelievable bills. And once in a while she'd go outside through the fire door, propping it open with her foot, lighting up with the other smokers.

Tuesday morning, Matt wrapped a schedule for the bus to Children's Memorial around a roll of quarters, shoved it into his pocket, and went to school. He found his name listed number two on the eighth-grade roster posted outside the athletic office.

He shrugged. Number two on a fourth-place team. How exciting. He drifted from class to class, listening politely as the teachers yakked about adverbial phrases of time, place, and manner; the triumph of Gothic architecture during the thirteenth century; prime numbers. After lunch, he tucked his glove under his stool and spent two hours in the science lab with Dr. Evers and the advanced biology students. Cell biology and intro genetics, nothing too hard.

By Thursday afternoon, the roll of quarters in his pocket was an irritating weight, slapping his leg with every step. Still, Matt kept it in his pocket. Because he was ready. Ready to visit Tom. That was the deal. One of these days after school, for sure. Just as soon as he whipped up the energy.

Because fourth-place ball practice was extremely tiring. It was exhausting, living up to all the expectations. The first time Matt strolled onto the field, he found Coach Pangbourn down on one knee in the grass between home plate and the mound, five baseballs palmed in her broad left hand. She was throwing dirt pitches to the catcher and making pointed comments about his short throws to second.

"Great. See Mr. Stine, Matt." Coach Pangbourn looked up briefly. "He's the dad who's helping us out with batting this year. Tell him to watch your right wrist."

Matt trotted toward the batting cages, feeling loose, feeling good. On the field again. All winter long he'd been waiting for the season to start, playing a little basketball, working out, biking to the hospital for visiting hours. Sometimes Tom had that first-floor room, and Matt would hitch Axle's leash to the handlebars and race that dumb dog past Tom's window. Tom would wave weakly and mouth, "Good boy, Axle. Good boy." Old Axle would go nuts. He'd lunge straight for the glass—dragging collar, leash, bike, boy, everything—frustrated beyond belief at being separated from his master. After that Matt would have to yank him home, mostly uphill on the return trip, fighting gravity and a fifty-pound dog. A great off-season workout. He'd stagger into the house, stand in front of the fridge, and gulp down Gatorade, trying to replace a bucket of sweat while Axle, outside in his kennel, would put up a despairing howl that lasted for hours.

"So you're the hitter from Amesville I've been hearing about?" asked the batting coach, interrupting Matt's thoughts. Matt shrugged modestly. "Good, good. Get a bat and helmet."

Matt picked a bat out of the rack. The bat handle had been wrapped with fresh grip tape. He tried to remember if anybody ever taped the grips fresh in Amesville and drew a blank. Didn't matter. He put on a helmet. Here was baseball, at last, in his hands.

His fingers curled around the handle. Weird. Didn't feel like baseball. Lifting the bat felt pointless and insane. Matt looked around the field. Bunches of idiot kids and coaches all over the field warming up. Catch, throw, run. Sick, married, baseball. What was he *doing* here?

Matt's grip tightened until his knuckles turned white. He crouched and took a couple of short, fierce practice swings. Calm down. Focus on the bat. The expensive bat of a fourth-place team. The fourth-place team he was going to lift out of the pack. Just one more part of the deal. That's all.

The batting coach was watching him. "I'm thinking you can tell us how to hit your pitcher," he said.

Matt blinked in astonishment. "Who, him?" he said, pointing his bat toward Upper West's rawboned pitching talent standing in front of the dugout.

The coach snorted. "Him? Forget him. I mean Amesville. We can't hit Amesville. Not that anybody else in the league can, either."

A couple of guys stopped swinging around and listened in. Matt shrugged. There wasn't much to tell. Tyler could kill opposing teams with strikeouts, but he was too much of a gentleman not to let the batters hit once in a while.

"Well," said Matt, "the one thing he won't tolerate is a batter crowding the plate. Stand in close, and you'll make him mad. Trust me, you do not want to make Tyler mad."

A couple more players wandered over and then a couple more. Matt looked up and found himself standing in the middle of a crowd.

"And?" said the coach eagerly. "What else?"

Matt rubbed his chin. "Well, sometimes Ross—the catcher—he'll sort of let you know the next pitch."

"Sure," said the first baseman sarcastically. "He says stuff like, 'Uh-oh. Tyler wants to throw a curve—'"

"'—you okay with that?'" the right fielder chimed in. Matt grinned. He got Ross's slow, matter-of-fact tone just right. "'Cause if you ain't, then I can back him off and call for something over the middle."

"Right in front of everybody he gets up and yells, 'Tyler! Hey, Ty, pitch something decent, and let this one hit it,'" continued the shortstop.

The first baseman kicked at the grass. "He sets down and says, 'It's gonna be fine, pal. Chest high and straight over.' And you're thinking, What kind of jerk does this guy think I am? So you dig in and swing for a low out-side curve. Ball comes in high and straight over. Best pitch of the game, and your bat whiffs six inches under."

There were murmurs all around. Matt grinned faint-ly, a little homesick. "Yeah. Good old Ross. He tells you the truth. Not that it helps."

The crowd broke up as the field coaches started call-ing out drills. Mrs. Pangbourn, on the mound, waved him over.

"Ready, Matt?" She scuffed the bag of balls at her feet. "Let's see what you got."

She threw a couple of warm-ups, then signaled him into the box. For a second, Matt felt the weight of the day, the field, the lady pitcher, the whistling breath of the sweating catcher, the strange faces on the field crammed down his throat, pinning the bat to his shoul-der. There was no way he could do this. No way in the world. The first pitch, low and outside, a pitcher's pitch, slapped into the catcher's mitt. Mrs. Pangbourn grinned, happy to have gotten that one past him.

By pure reflex, Matt lifted his bat—and everything fell into place: the day, the lady pitcher, everything. On the second pitch, he leaned back on his heels and brought the bat around for his traditional swing-and-a-miss. For humility. For luck.

The onlookers hooted.

"Way back on your heels, son," called the batting coach.

"Hey, you suck," said the catcher, all surprised. "You're not supposed to suck."

Matt ignored them all, even the that-was-easy smirk on Coach Pangbourn's face. A cocky look for a pitcher to have after only two pitches. A look he was going to wipe off with his bat, most definitely.

She threw, and Matt brought his hands around so quick, so clean, the bat was the silken blur of a Japanese fan opening and closing with the flick of his wrists. Line drive, deep left, a nice solid *thump* as it hit the turf smack in the middle of a pop-fly drill.

"Heads up!" barked the fielding coach. A kid picked it up and threw the ball infield.

"One out. Runner on second. He takes a small lead-off because he's slow and a weenie. Get him to third, Matt," called Coach Pangbourn.

Matt could see the play. Catcher, probably, out there on second, still wheezing from the run, wondering if he's going to have a heart attack. Second baseman shifts right; center fielder shuffles his feet in the gap like he's going to back up the base but stays out, drifts left—and there's his mistake. Too bad, so sad. Matt loaded and launched the ball knee high. It dropped two feet behind the lumbering phantom catcher's trailing leg, just out of reach of an imaginary diving center fielder caught playing too deep.

Mrs. Pangbourn and the batting coach exchanged a giddy look of happiness. "Oh, yeah, it's baseball, Bob!" yelled Mrs. Pangbourn.

"His wrist doesn't look so bad to me," he yelled back.

"Keep watching," said Mrs. Pangbourn.

"Swing for the fences, son," urged the batting coach. And Matt did. Over and over and over again.

"Mercy," yelled Coach Pangbourn finally. She wiped the sweat out of her cap. "I'm gonna sit over there in the shade and groan."

She put her cap back on and looked Matt over. "The boy can hit. The boy can field. And he's mine, all mine." She rubbed her hands together, gloating.

The batting coach turned to Matt. "After a couple of hits, you start turning your right wrist in the follow-through. It's a good snap—for throwing a bowling ball." He looked Matt over. "I believe we can help you with that."

And so, every afternoon for the next two weeks, Matt wrapped his hands around a bat and extended and snapped his right wrist until his forearm tingled pleasantly. Until the team lined up at home plate for running drills, sprinting to beat the shortstop's bang-bang throw to first base. Coach Pangbourn called the play.

"Safe," she said as the runners passed. "Safe. Safe.

You're out. This is a sprint, Adam. Sprint means to run quickly. Safe. Safe. Jeez, Marco, you're sliding into first here? Two outs for stupidity."

They circled and ran again. Matt, taller than most, quicker than most, made all his runs. "Good. Good, Matt."

Upper West's regular season opened on a Tuesday afternoon with a home game against Grove City. During warmups, Matt kept glancing at the stands, sort of expecting his family to show up and claim that big, sunny spot in the front-row bleachers—a good place to spread out with blankets and lawn chairs and the dented cooler full of iced tea and grape juice. Ashley would get out the juice. Kelsey would hand around the cups. His mom and dad would be laughing and talking, getting ready to yell their lungs out.

Dylan would shoot over to the dugout. He'd hang around until Matt kicked him back to the stands. Then he'd climb to the top of the bleachers and sit with Tom, the two of them horsing around until Marianne, off from work, got there and made them behave.

"Go, Matt. Get a hit." That was all Tom ever said. But he said it at every up, every inning, every game. Didn't matter if they were down by two or up by nine— Tom understood the nature of the game. The idea was to win. Winning meant your team crossed home plate a whole lot more than the opposing team. Getting that far meant you had runners in scoring position—second base was fine; third, even finer. Scoring position meant you got on base. Getting on base meant a hit. A fine, fast hit.

A fat lady and her kids moved into the sunny spot on the bleachers. Matt stopped looking.

He trotted out to the field as the pitcher took the hill. Matt squared up and rolled to the balls of his feet, squinting a little at the powerful sight of an infield on the edge of play. His glove whispered to him as he stretched out his hands in front of him, watching the pitcher wind up. "Ready. Ready—"

Matt shook his head. Shame, a guy like that pitching in the same league as Ty Smith. Upper West's jerky windup looked like one of those plastic action figures Dylan got in his Happy Meals. Pitiful. Matt had a horrible thought: What the heck kind of field chatter backs up a pitcher who can't pitch? "Hum it, hum it in, rock and fire, yah yah, rocket fire" was gonna sound fake and sarcastic rolled out for a guy whose curveball never curved.

"Ball," called the umpire.

Matt glanced around the field. He wasn't the only one having problems coming up with some encouragement. The ump's voice was the first on the field. Everybody else was laying low. Coach Pangbourn, yakking on her cell phone in the dugout, looked resigned to starting the season with a pitch that missed the plate.

Jeez. If there was ever a pitcher who needed a little up talk, Upper West's sure did. The guy's shoulders were touching his ears, practically, as he threw the next pitch.

"Ball," called the ump again. "Two and oh." Grove City's dugout erupted in catcalls and clappings. "Wait for your pitch, Jeremy!" they yelled, which was short-hand for "The guy's gonna walk you, Jeremy. Wait him out."

Matt crouched over his glove, pounding the pocket meditatively with his throwing hand, thinking about it. Two pitches into the season, and he could already see fourth-place thunderclouds looming over the pitcher's head. He watched another discouraged windup.

Matt opened his mouth. "Yep," he yelled. "Yep, yep, yep."

He winced. As chatter it was beyond pathetic, but the left fielder, a smart guy with a quick glove who deserved a better team, picked it right up. "Yep," he bellowed to the first baseman.

The first baseman pawed the dirt with his tag foot and brought up his glove, ready. "Yep, yep, *yep,*" came his voice, big and loud and sure. It echoed off the dugout, ricocheted into right field, and suddenly the bases and outfield crackled "Yep. Yep yep yep"—like firecrackers. Like flamethrowers. "Yep yep hum yep"— like a firestorm.

Coach Pangbourn put down her phone, a little surprised to hear the team chatter, but ready to run with it. *"Yep,"* she roared back, and the benchers behind her took it up like a chant. *"Yep, yep, yep-yep-yep-yep-yep-yep . . ."*

The pitcher's shoulders came off his ears. He crouched and threw.

"Hee-*rike!*" boomed the ump.

"Cool," said the left fielder to Matt.

"Very cool," agreed Matt. "Yep, yep, YEP."

Grove City scored a couple of runs in the first inning before their batter tipped a foul back to Upper West's catcher for the third out. Upper West's lead batters singled and ran the bases just right, so when Matt came up at three bat, he had no outs and the tying runs on first and third.

Just great.

Matt set up in the box. He crouched, waiting.

"Go, Matt. Get a hit," he murmured.

"You say something?" asked Grove City's catcher as the pitcher threw, and Matt swung. A nice up and out to left field that sat down fair and bounced foul. A hit impossible to field with any dignity, the kind of hit Matt gloried in. Power under full control. Sure enough, Grove City's left fielder, red-faced and panting, threw it into third as Upper West's one and two hitters cruised home. The base coach waved Matt to a stop at second.

"Nice hit," he called.

The first of several nice hits. Matt went three for four. Nothing big, nothing fancy, but with his swing whispering good things about the season ahead, it was a fine game. Upper West won, seven to three.

"Good game," Coach Pangbourn said to him. "Very good game, Matt."

Matt nodded, suddenly tired. The stands were filled with strangers, the chatter was pathetic, but he had hit, he had fielded, a very good game. Holding up his end of the deal.

He rode the late bus to the Harrisons' house, lugging a gym bag full of books up to Rickey Harrison's room. He came downstairs, microwaved another burrito, ate it over the sink, popped a few cookies in his mouth. Then he spent the rest of the silent evening upstairs at Rickey Harrison's desk, working on class assignments, staring until the print blurred, and it was eleven o'clock. His mom was still at the hospital.

When the phone rang, Matt jumped a mile.

"So, how'd it go?" asked his mom.

"We won. Seven to three."

"Hey, hey." He heard her lighter click on. She inhaled. "Whatcha up to?"

"Math."

"Homework? You're doing homework after a game? You're kidding, right?"

"Huh-uh."

"Jesus God almighty, Matt." She exhaled sharply, smoke whistling over the mouthpiece. "You okay?"

"Sure." He stuck the phone between his ear and shoulder and started scanning his answers. "How is he?"

There was a pause. His mom cleared her throat. "He's kind of out of it right now," she said carefully. "Think I'll hang around here tonight. You know."

Matt's heart sank a little. His mom had developed that real careful tone of voice over the past couple of months. It meant that Tom wasn't doing so hot. That there were complications. Of course, all Matt said was "Okay."

"You sure?"

"Sure I'm sure." Matt wanted to help her out. He wanted to say something brave and confident, something like "Yep yep, Mom, yep, not much longer, and he'll be done with it," but for the first time since Tom got sick, the backup chatter got stuck in his throat.

"Okay. There's plenty of cereal for breakfast." There was another pause. "Truth is, it's bad, Matt. It's real bad. I don't know. Maybe you should wait until next week to visit. When Dad comes up."

"Okay." Matt bent over his paper, working hard. He erased an answer; penciled in a new one; erased that one, too. His mom said it was real bad. . . . She'd never said that before. He felt like slamming his head against

Rickey Harrison's wall. "That works. I need to stick around here pretty close. School is tough, and Coach isn't cutting me any slack."

"Next week for sure, though," whispered his mom. "When Dad comes up."

His pencil moved roughly over the paper, erasing, filling in, keeping up his end of the deal. "Sure thing. Next week, when Dad comes up."

He hung up the phone, enormously relieved. He was off the hook until next week. And a week, a whole week, that was good. Not that he was looking for an excuse, right? He wasn't running away from his part of the deal or anything. It was just the way things were working out.

Matt took the bus schedule and roll of quarters out of his pocket and set them carefully on the corner of Rickey Harrison's desk. No sense in carrying this stuff around for the next week or so. And they'd be safe here. Safe and sound, yep yep yep.

# 6

## AWAY GAME

**TWO** days later, Matt's dad left a message on the Harrisons' voice mail. Matt listened to it as he microwaved a frozen burrito.

"I got some bad news, babe. Ashley and Dylan both spiked a fever last night—"

"Mommy? I got a headache," wheezed Dylan into the extension.

"—so I took them to the clinic this morning. Acute bronchitis, both of 'em. The doc said for goodness' sake don't go anywhere near Tom—"

"That's when Daddy said a bad word," croaked Dylan. "Verrrry bad."

"—or anyone that might have contact with him. So we're gonna have to stay put. I'm on evenings mostly this week—"

"Hi, Mommy. It's me, Ashley."

"—so Kelsey and me are okay with her school hours and everything. Boy, Kelsey deserves a medal after last night. But it leaves you two up there alone holding it together—"

"I miss you, Mommy."

"—you and Matt."

"I'm trying real hard not to cough. We're sorry we got sick, Mommy. We didn't mean to. Bye-yah, Mommy. Dylan says bye-yah, too."

"Matt? Help your mom out."

"I want to say bye-yah my own self," complained Dylan. "Bye, Mommy. And remember, you can't tell Matt about the surprise, 'kay?"

The machine announced the date and time and clicked off. "Oh, man, Dad," murmured Matt, a little homesick at hearing his dad's voice again. "You missed her by five minutes."

His mom had left early that morning. It was April 10. Transplant day. The day Tom was having his harvested bone marrow replanted in hopes that it would grow and reproduce cancer-free. Dripped intravenously through the well-used venous port implanted next to his left armpit.

Matt checked the clock. Past seven-thirty. No doubt his mom would stay at the hospital tonight. Just another frozen burrito and cookie night. He opened the freezer and got out two more packages. He was starving. He'd just gotten home himself, off the late bus from

Zanesville, where Upper West Bexley had played its first away game.

Matt put his plate in the microwave and grinned, thinking about it. The game had turned into a real batting romp. In the second inning, he had hit a line drive that popped out of the right fielder's glove. The guy picked it up and then dropped it while Matt burned around the bases for a triple, and the dugout hooted and hollered, "Yep, Matt, yep." After that, they couldn't miss. Even Upper West's catcher had made it to first base with a soft lob into left. And when Upper West's catcher started base hitting . . . Matt shook his head in wonder at what passed for defense in Zanesville.

He popped a couple of cookies in his mouth as he tried to figure out why, in a game that promised nothing but good things for the season, he had started hearing voices in center field. Not bad, scary voices whispering about a jump off the I-70 bridge or anything insane like that. Just voices he had heard most of his life saying plain, everyday stuff.

He had heard Marianne's voice, the way she sounded when he and Tom dropped by the nursing home to say hiya. Like she'd just taken senile old Mr. Jackson's wheelchair grips in her small, freckled hands and popped a wheelie over the humpy threshold of the main door. *"Now, Mr. Jackson,"* she said in Matt's ear—right there, out in center field, bottom of the fourth. Shallow left center. From the dugout, Coach Pangbourn kept trying to wave him deeper.

*"Now, Mr. Jackson,"* said Marianne's voice, *"it's another pretty day. Hold your face up to the sun. Like that. Don't that feel good? Just another real pretty day."*

Matt had looked up, felt the sun on his face, as Zanesville's first batter popped up to left center. Real, real shallow. Didn't have to shuffle his feet, even, to catch it. "Yep yep YEP" crackled gleefully around the field, but he could still hear Mrs. Pangbourn's annoyed sigh all the way from the dugout.

He pegged the ball to the shortstop and watched the infield move it around the bases. *"Least we'll have one decent player to hit to,"* commented Ross's voice in Matt's other ear.

Ross was most certainly that minute riding bus forty-three home down Scatter Ridge, choking on all the travel grit kicked up on the back roads. Ross always opened the window before he sat down. It was hot in the back of the bus.

"Upper West Bexley's got some decent players," said Matt out loud. "You don't lock up fourth place in a tough league by sitting on your hands."

*"Uh-huh,"* said the voice. It sounded like Ross might be leaning against the left-field fence and had to raise his voice a little to be heard. *"They hang around in the*

*back of the box and watch Tyler's fast balls go by. They get a guy on first, and their bench goes crazy thinkin' he's gonna steal second on the next pitch. Like they haven't watched me throw the runner out at second every single time he—"*

Upper West's pitcher—Jason? Jordan?—threw. Called strike.

"See there?" murmured Matt. "See that pitch? Caught the sun real pretty, just like Tyler's curve."

*"Uh-huh. Catcher missed it, though. You don't see me scrabbling around in the dirt like that. Well. Least you're up there. We'll have one decent player to hit to,"* repeated Ross's voice. *"When we travel up in May to beat Upper West. Them and their hand-poured, custom-made titanium bats."*

On a one-two pitch, the second Zanesville batter got nervous and took a big chop at the ball. It bounced into the pitcher's glove, an easy throw to first. Two gone. Matt folded his glove under his arm, bent down, and wiped his fingers in the cool, dense grass.

"Matt! Straight out!" yelled Coach Pangbourn. "I mean it!" Matt trotted backward and settled down deep in center field.

There was just one more voice that inning—the faint, dark voice of Tom. The same voice the day Matt had walked into their bedroom holding out the last can of ginger ale. Tom's bed was empty. Tom's bed was empty because Tom was in the bathroom, hands and knees on the tile floor, throwing up a thin river of blood and bile into a grass-green towel.

*"Don't tell Mom,"* said the voice wetly as the batter swung and sent a fast hop into left field. The fielder scooped up the ball and nailed the runner at first. Three up, three down.

*"Don't tell Mom,"* repeated Tom. *"She'll kill me for ruining her towel."*

Matt stood in the kitchen in his dirty ball uniform, staring blindly at the microwave, the sink, the cookie crumbs on the floor, feeling just a little dizzy. Everything was fine, fine, really. The game had been an easy win for Upper West. But it made him tired, suddenly, thinking about those voices in center field. One more thing to deal with.

# 7

## BATTING SLUMP

**A** couple of days later in the dugout, fifth inning, Upper West hosting Lancaster, Coach Pangbourn's cell phone rang. She answered it and started spluttering.

"Where did you get this phone number?" she demanded. "Oh. I see. Yeah, tell him hello. Of course you won." Coach rubbed her nose, trying to hide her grin. "They were nine and seven last year, and from everything I hear, they're not doing any better this year." Her glance cut over to Matt. She squinted at him like she'd never seen him before.

"Sure. He's right here." Coach held out the phone to Matt. Matt took it.

"Hello?"

"So. You winnin' or losin'?" came Ross's voice, loud and clear over the phone.

"Hey, I been thinking about you," said Matt easily. "How'd you know where I was?"

"Aw, easy. Coach gave me the league schedule with

all the other coaches' cell phone numbers. He's making me use my phone card so I don't roam out of his network or something."

"Cool," said Matt.

"Yeah. I tried calling you a bunch of times at the mansion, but all I get is voice mail. So anyway, we just finished up here against Newark. Eleven–eight. We pulled it out, but the game ran a whole lot closer than last year. Coach is kind of upset."

Coach Quinn was yelling in the background. "Tell that boy to get back home and hit where he belongs, Berg!" Matt grinned.

"Hey, Matt," said Coach Pangbourn, her eyes on the game, "wind it up. You're next on deck."

"Gotta go, Ross."

"What you hittin' so far?"

"What, this game? Couple of singles."

"Nah, what's your season?"

"It's good. Still hanging up there." Actually, six games into the season and his batting average was .693, but he was pretty sure it was bad luck, spouting off your early-days average over a cell phone. "Coach is pretty happy."

Ross groaned. "Todd Striker's at .209. He's screwed up every throw to home he's tried. Coach is talking about trading Striker for Ashley Bradshaw. Remember her? She's the center fielder on the girls' softball team. Plus she can relief pitch."

"Whoa," said Matt, totally satisfied. Todd was working out even worse than he had hoped.

"Okay, sure, so maybe Ashley'd play better than Todd, but *nobody* wants to face life with a girl in center field. Believe me, you can't get back here soon enough," said Ross.

"Matt! Let's go!" Coach threw him a batting helmet. "Get a hit."

"How's your brother, Matt?" asked Ross. "Matt?"

Matt didn't answer. Ross's question tumbled through the dugout air as he flipped the phone back to Coach Pangbourn and headed to the plate.

Because, to be honest, he didn't know how his brother was. To be honest, he couldn't figure out how it was he hadn't gone to see Tom. The roll of quarters and the bus schedule were still on the corner of Rickey Harrison's desk, he was pretty sure, so it wasn't like he was *never* going downtown. It was just that he hadn't yet. No big deal. He'd get around to it. He dug into the box, raised the bat, and waited. In the meantime, things were good. He was hanging on to a C+ in English. Upper West was in third place, solid. His mom was at the hospital, taking care of Tom while Matt played baseball. See? Everything under control.

Matt crouched and swung. Picture-perfect shot, deep right, the fielder caught playing close to center, charging after the ball, wondering how the heck a hit like that came off the swing of a big right-hander. Two runs batted in. Matt grinned to himself as he scuffed up the dirt around third base and took a little leadoff. Maybe Ross would call back. He could sort of mention the hit.

And then, over the next couple of games, disaster struck. Four weeks into the regular season, Matt hit into a batting slump. Pop-ups. Grounders to first. Line drives turned straight into double plays, all sorts of crazy stuff. The power was there, sort of, but he had totally lost control of the bat.

At first, Coach Pangbourn wasn't worried. "Shake it off, Matt," she called from the first-base line as his foul tip backflipped neatly into the catcher's mitt in the game against New Lexington. She said it again as he hit a line drive directly into the shortstop's glove. Upper West lost, a real heartbreaker, six to eight. "Shake it off."

He just couldn't figure it out. By mid-season he was always cranked up, brushing aside the defense with crafty little drops into right that scored the runner on third; short balls that ran the foul line over third and stayed fair; then, when the outfield played close, thinking he'd lost strength, he'd uncork the Big Hit—straight out, ball screaming toward the center-field fence, outfield scrambling like idiots, while he ran the bases in glory.

But instead of a mid-season bat that felt like a nail stuck in an electric socket, it felt . . . cold, metal, hollow, disconnected. A bat like that made no sense. And everything he hit turned into a fluke, a freak, an accident.

Coach Pangbourn tried to remain calm, but Matt knew she was getting chopped. "Shake it off, Matt," she barked as he popped up to the first baseman in the game against Newark. As he popped up to the third baseman. As he popped up to the pitcher. "C'mon, shake it off."

Upper West lost: seven to fourteen.

"We'll shake it off," said Coach Pangbourn semiconfidently in the bus going home. "We're still in third place." Her glance cut over to Matt. "More or less."

Fortunately, his glove was as quick as ever. It saved Upper West in the game against Springfield. Matt threw out two different base runners at home from right center, which made him MVP. (One of his throws missed the Upper West's pitcher's left ear by three inches. Coach Pangbourn was right, Matt noticed. Kid shook like a leaf for the rest of the game.) But they lost a couple of close games. Scraped up a win. Then lost a couple more. All because Matt couldn't move the ball.

Coach Pangbourn grabbed him in the hallway right after the dismissal bell.

"You're shaking it, right, Matt?" Her voice was full of hope. "You look like you're shaking it. Yeah, you look good. You look real good. Shaking it and everything. Good. Good job."

She passed a hand before her eyes. "Yikes. Sorry, Matt. Sorry I'm breathing down your neck like this. It's just that we're so close to putting a lock on third. I'm a little anxious." She took a deep breath and looked at the ceiling. "Shake it off, Coach Pangbourn," she mumbled to the lights.

Her cell phone rang. She answered it, still staring at the ceiling.

"Hi, Ross. Yep, nice to hear your voice, too. What is this, the third call this week? Uh-huh. Uh-huh. As a matter of fact, he's standing right here." She handed the phone to Matt. "Give me the phone back at practice," she muttered, and stalked away.

"So you're in trouble, right? In the principal's office and everything, huh?" said Ross, real happiness in his voice. "She's gonna kick you off the team or something, and then we have no worries about Upper West's outfield, right?"

Matt grinned. "You're really starting to bug her, you know? She's got this nasty twitch in one eye." Ross just laughed.

He didn't tell Ross about the slump, though. Not in that conversation, not the next, and not the next after that. Because it wasn't like it was a big deal or anything. Just a little cold bat, nothing to worry about. He could handle it. His head was still in the game.

So day after day, he ground his spikes into the dirt

and clutched up and worked on his wrists, or stayed on the knob and worked on his wrists, or jogged into the outfield, thinking about his wrists. Even at night in the Harrisons' empty house, lying in bed and listening to the rain pattering against the diamond-paned windows, he worked on it. Went over and over his stance, his load, his launch, thought about it with the sick feeling in his gut that everything was completely right—a picture-perfect hitting sequence—and still his bat was passing the plate in some kind of freaking fourth-place softball swing. Wrong, wrong, wrong.

His bat was falling to pieces. Unbelievable. How was he supposed to carry Upper West out of fourth place into something better without a bat?

An odd, random thought struck him—was that roll of bus quarters still on top of Rickey Harrison's desk? He opened his eyes and tried to see, but the rain had made the room so dark. He was too tired to get up. Tomorrow. He'd look tomorrow.

Or the next day, for sure. He couldn't let himself get sucked into all that other stuff before he took care of this slump. That was the deal. Focus, focus. When his hitting was back, everything would work out great. Upper West would be in third place. And finding that lousy roll of quarters wouldn't matter, because Tom would be better, be on his way home. And everything would work out great yep, yep. Just a little while longer.

Wearily, Matt closed his eyes. The bat was the main thing. Everything else would have to wait.

Along with working on his wrists and slumping ever deeper at the plate, Matt kept busy. He went to school. He did his homework. He hooked up with the left fielder, whose dad was the batting coach, and the three of them went to see a movie about outer space. Another time he cut through a bunch of backyards and terraced gardens and the seventh hole at the country club to Alum Creek, running pretty high for May. He sat and threw some rocks for a while. He slept late. He changed Rickey Harrison's sheets.

The best way to deal with the piles of stuff everywhere in Rickey Harrison's bedroom, Matt had found, was to keep the overhead light strictly off. He rigged a forty-watt clamp light to the brass bedstead and adjusted it to shine just over his right shoulder as he lounged against the pillows. A small, homey circle of yellow light fell on his hands and the pages of a book. Tom had a light like that, clamped to his bed back home. Stretched out on his bed every night, reading, looking up and smiling faintly as Matt nagged him to turn off the light and go to sleep. *"Give it a rest, Mommy."*

That was what Matt was doing—reading—the night his mom came home early from the hospital. She turned on the overhead light and sat on the edge of the bed.

"Whatcha reading?" She pushed up the cover of the

book with two fingers. "*Catcher in the Rye,* huh? Doesn't that have a lot of cussing in it?"

Matt rolled his eyes.

"Yeah. Well. I guess you pretty much heard all those words already." She stuck a cigarette in her mouth but didn't light it. Her fingers picked between the furrows on the green corduroy bedspread.

"Tom's doing okay," she said finally. "Better."

Matt cleared his throat. He hadn't spoken to a soul all day, and his voice was rusty. "Two steps forward, one step back."

"What?"

He studied his mom's face, the bitter lines at her mouth. "We got to write this expository paragraph. In English. About something we had in our life that went two steps forward and one step back."

His mom smiled grimly. "He's not throwing up so much, and he sleeps three whole hours at a time. So I guess that's the two steps forward." She looked up. "Tomorrow's Sunday. Nothing stopping you from coming with me to the hospital for a while tomorrow. We could visit the Harrisons' church in the morning. Sit in the back and sing some hymns. We haven't been to church once since we moved up here."

"Church'd be okay."

"But not the hospital, huh?" She examined the tip of her cigarette. "I could make you go. Haul your butt

**85**

right out of this bed and stuff you in the car. You'd be in Tommy's room saying hello before you knew what hit you."

She grimaced at her tired reflection in the mirrored closet door. "This hospital is real nice. Not like the county hospital. Remember? You'd walk in and about keel over at the smell of old ladies' perfume and Pine-Sol."

"That first-floor room they kept putting him in." Matt rubbed his shoulder, feeling Axle yank it out of the socket. "The cracks in the ceiling looked like an alligator."

"Weekdays, the hospital cafeteria closed up tight after lunch. I'd have to sneak you in a couple of meatloaf sandwiches for supper. You'd stash 'em under that ratty old chair next to the windows."

Matt smiled faintly. "They always tasted like Pine-Sol."

"Every day at three forty-five, right after school, there you'd be, coming into Tom's room holding your nose and asking Tom when he was going to stop goofing off."

"Yeah."

"Yeah."

"Yeah."

She sighed. "Who am I trying to kid? Don't matter how new the carpet is, this hospital's as horrible as that one. Bad enough *he's* got to suffer—"

She broke off, her chin trembling, hands fisting blindly into the bedspread. Matt stared down at the book in his hands, reading the same sentence over and over so he wouldn't have to look up and see his mom's face falling to pieces.

His mom swallowed. "Bad enough he's got to suffer without inflicting it on you," she whispered.

He tried to imagine Tom not barfing, dozing off in another hospital bed, in another hospital room. He tried to imagine Tom getting better—and drew a blank. His imagination about the future was wearing pretty thin lately. Of course, he didn't say that. He couldn't say anything like that. He didn't say anything at all.

His mom went back to chewing on her cigarette and smoothing out the bedspread. "So. How you doing?" she asked after a while.

"Okay."

"Okay?"

"Sure. Okay. Everything's . . ." Matt's voice trailed off as he rummaged through his brain, trying to figure out how he was doing. He was, he was . . . "Okay. Fine. Doing good."

"Yep," she said, getting off the bed and nudging his shoulder in the process. "We're all doing good."

After she left, Matt tried to get back to the book, but his eyes began to close. He turned off the light and got under the covers.

On Monday before school, Matt slapped something together for English. His paragraph, "Two Steps Forward and One Step Back," used a lot of weak verbs and trailing sentences to describe how he had learned to ride his bicycle way back when he was four years old. He got a C+. *Somewhat plodding and mechanical*, wrote Mrs. Tinker across the top in green ink.

In biology, he and a girl named Emily were reproducing Gregor Mendel's classic genetics experiment on pea plants. Emily had quite the green thumb. Pea plants filled the windowsills and twined along the table legs and grew so fast Matt had to get down on his hands and knees and scrounge around in the moist green jungle under the table for his stashed fielder's mitt. No, he was doing okay with stuff at school. Things only got a little weird during baseball.

Mrs. Pangbourn pulled him into the corner of the dugout during warmups before the Pickerington game. "I'm moving you to number five in the batting order," she said.

Matt shrugged. He had been expecting it.

Mrs. Pangbourn stuck her hand in her back pocket. "I'm thinking your slump is pretty understandable, Matt. You've transferred in the middle of the school year. You're under a lot of stress. Strange living conditions, different coaching styles, your brother's illness." She waited. Matt shrugged again.

Mrs. Pangbourn rocked slowly on her heels. "You know, the more I think about it, the less the cold bat worries me. I've got bigger things on my mind. Like what I'm hearing from the teachers about you. 'Quiet, well behaved, polite. Really settled down in class. Wish we had a school full of kids like him.'"

She snorted. "Quiet, well behaved? *Polite?*" Her mouth pruned up, like what the teachers were saying was the lousiest kind of putdown instead of a bunch of praise. "What happened to the cocky kid with the tie lounging around in my office last month? The kid who beat us up so bad with his bat last year?"

"He's slumping," muttered Matt.

"Yeah? Slumping—or sinking?" She leaned over, set his ball cap from front to back and looked him deep in the eye. "Okay, Matt, I'm gonna ask a direct question here. How are you doing? Hanging in there? Or going down for the third time?"

Matt rotated his right shoulder and thought about that. Here was the basic problem with having a girl as head coach. Girls psyched up before a game by having a nice chat about relationships. Guys maintained an intense silence in which they got ready to drag the opposing players across the field by their pointy little ears. So Coach dropped him to fifth bat and wanted to discuss feelings? Okay, sure. The feeling he wanted most to discuss was the one where he felt like dropping a couple of hand-poured, custom-made titanium bats on Mrs. Pangbourn's foot.

Fortunately, the umpire hit the play button just then, and "The Star Spangled Banner" boomed out of a tape player. Matt took off his backward cap and laid it respectfully over his heart. Then he set it on his head the right way and trotted wordlessly out to center field, where those crazy voices were waiting for him.

"*I notice,*" said Tom's voice in Matt's ear as the Pickerington batter whiffed the ball straight into the third baseman's glove. "*I notice that you've been playing on this team for a month, and you still don't know anybody's name.*"

"Do so," murmured Matt. "That pitcher's name is Jason. Or Jordan. Something. And that kid in left field is the batting coach's son. I'll think of his name in a minute."

"*Like I should talk. There's this one oncologist who's been my case handler since the day after I got here. He's got to be almost as young as me; he's up close and personal with the night nurse, if you know what I mean—and I just can't get the guy's name. In my mind, I call him Dr. Chance.*"

Bat two hit a nice grounder to short, who muffed it. With the runner on first, the three bat hit a slow hop into center field. Matt scooped up the ball and underhanded it to second base. The runner was short and quick. There he was, smirking, standing up safe at second.

"And I know the pea plant girl's name for sure," Matt said as he backed deep into center field. Fourth batter, real power, and a switch-hitter to boot. He felt a twinge of heartfelt jealousy. He crouched down, ready to go left or right. "Her name is Emily."

The batter banged it over the short left-field fence. His heartfelt jealousy turned to pea-green envy. "I gotta go now, Tom. I gotta concentrate."

*"Yeah, okay. Bye-yah."*

*"We meant it, Mrs. Bainter. What we promised each other. We meant it forever."*

"Come on, Marianne," muttered Matt impatiently. "Clear the field."

At the bottom of the first, the dugout was packed with faces carefully turned away as he dropped onto the bench to wait. Fifth. He'd never batted so far down the order before. Fifth. Fifth. He always hit in the first inning. Always. But the chatter was not for him. His gut started to burn.

"C'mon, Adam, let's go!" shouted voices to the lead-off. "Let's go, go!"

Matt clenched his fingers, flexed them, rotated his wrists. The pitcher, Jason Jordan Somebody, sat down next to him.

"They'll hit you up," he said hesitantly, like he wasn't half the player Matt was, when the truth was he was turning out to be this season's talent. "You'll get up."

But Matt didn't. Upper West retired with one on base. Matt trotted out to the field, the rage in his gut tearing up his concentration. "*Listen, you can borrow any of my stuff. If you want to.*"

The plays kept rolling, but his timing was off, his edge gone. A high pop-up. Matt fumbled the ball out of his glove and threw to home. The runner beat it by three strides.

"C'mon, Matt!" yelled the catcher. "Shake it up!"

"*You happy, Matt?*" asked Marianne softly.

Running the center-field fence, sun in his eyes.

"*Matt?*" said Ross's voice quietly. "*You okay?*"

"I'll be home in time for play-offs," mumbled Matt, crow-hopping into a bad throw from the warning track.

"C'mon, Matt, hit the cutoff! Open your eyes out there!" bellowed Mrs. Pangbourn.

His bat gone, his glove falling to pieces, and Upper West lost it, five to four. Matt walked out of the dugout alone, sweating like a pig.

Mrs. Pangbourn stopped him in the gym. "Bad game," she said. "The worst kind. We played to lose."

Matt said nothing. He pushed open the locker-room door.

"Matt," called Mrs. Pangbourn. She stood in the middle of the darkened gym, watching him. "We're two games out of third place. Two lousy games. I'd sure like to sweep this weekend series of three. You know who we're playing starting tomorrow, right?"

Matt shook his head. Mrs. Pangbourn gave him a long, considering look.

"Amesville, Matt. We're playing Amesville Middle School."

## 8

## MAXIMUM WRIST SNAP

**THAT** night, in the yellow glow of the forty-watt light, Matt took up his batter's stance in front of the full-length mirror on Rickey Harrison's closet door. Hopeless, he knew that. He could feel it in the air. But he had to try, right? Try and try and try. Numbly, he choked up on a hockey stick above the Chicago Black Hawks emblem and waggled it in the air.

"Maximum wrist snap," he murmured. The hockey stick swished through the air.

"Shoulder down, hip weight back, stride foot. Throw the bat at the ball." Matt looked in the mirror at the pale-faced, sweating guy with a cocked hockey stick over his right shoulder.

The guy in the mirror had a terrible stance—way tense. Not a kid's stance, all happy and open with hips straight on toward the pitcher. And not the stance of a wise old man, bent over and devious, trying to hide a big strike zone. Who was he, that guy in the mirror?

A guy about to be humiliated by his ice-cold bat. His swing-and-a-miss in ballparks all over central Ohio witnessed by the near strangers on Upper West's team had been bad enough. Now the humiliation would be total. In front of guys he had known since way before this past year. The one with the big hole blown in it by sickness and surgery and treatment.

Matt cocked the hockey stick. His head throbbed. It had to be a bad sign, that whispering behind him. The center-field voices had followed him home.

*"Let him sleep. He's exhausted,"* whispered his mother's husky voice. *"He never stops. He's there anytime Tom needs something, or yells for help, or just plain yells, period."*

*"This is gonna break his heart,"* murmured his dad.

Matt clenched the hockey stick. His knuckles turned red, then white. The face of the guy in the mirror sprang out ugly and hateful. Matt stared the stranger down as the stick drove again and again at the ball. Two hockey sticks whistling through the air, cutting, chopping. Two pale faces, twisting into masks. Two voices, rising in the silence.

*"Bet you fifty bucks,"* said Tom's voice.

"Part of the deal, right?" panted Matt. "Not fall to pieces."

*"Bet you fifty more bucks."*

"Not blow up the universe, starting with Rickey Harrison's IDIOT hockey stick!"

*"Atta boy, Matt."*

Matt clenched his teeth and whispered, "We have to be tough." *"Go get 'em."*

"We have to bat .380 and field every ball and back up Tom—*"Atta boy atta boy fire it in there fire it in rocket hum"*—because if we don't, *"If we don't—"*

The last perfect swing touched the beveled edge of the mirror. Kissed the surface, inside and outside. A chip of glass tinkled to the floor. Matt dropped the hockey stick and froze, breathless. Silent. Hearing just one voice now. Just one.

My voice. The voice I used to say over and over *"Everything's great. Great, really, fine, fine."* I've said it so many times that things either have to start going great, or I cut the crap.

And the one thing that had always been great, the one last thing I knew for sure about—hitting a baseball—was being sucked down the same drain as my brother's life. I'd never hit the ball again, thanks to his stupid, stupid, stupid cancer—

I picked up the stick and swung hard. That hockey stick flamed past the edge of the closet. Bashed the glass into fifty pieces. The guy in the mirror never stood a chance.

I dropped the stick on the floor. Good thing Tom's already dying. Good thing. Otherwise I'd have to kill him.

# 9

## DUSTED BACK

**THE** next morning I put on my shoes and kicked the bigger chunks of mirror out of my way. I toed up a couple of quarters. Sometime in the last month, that roll of bus quarters had dropped off the edge of Rickey Harrison's desk and split open. I had never noticed.

Didn't matter. I'd clean it up after the game. That sharp, edgy, ten-dollars-in-quarters mess all over the floor would be my good-luck charm for game one against Amesville. I went downstairs, shaking my head. A full-length mirror, jeez. Stupid thing to have in your room.

"Tom moved to a step-down unit last night, moved down to the ninth floor; he's doing that good," chirped Mom at breakfast. "How 'bout you and Ross take the bus to the hospital after the game, and I take you out for pizza? We'll put a piece in a napkin for Tom."

Oh yeah? So he gets better and I get a batting slump? I get to look like a jerk holding a cold bat, and he gets a piece of my pizza? Of course, I couldn't say stuff like that. Think stuff like that. Hate him like that. It wasn't his fault. He was sick. I was well enough to have a batting slump.

Mom winked at me. "Besides, there's gonna be a little surprise for you this afternoon."

Great. Like was she actually going to do me a favor and show up at the game? The cornflakes tasted like gravel.

Mom called Dad with the news about Tom while I finished my bowl of gravel and headed out the door for the bus.

I sat under the skylights in remedial English, learning the use of linking verbs.

Hello, my name *is* Matthew Bainter.

My batting average for the Upper West Bexley Wildcats *remains* .193.

My brother *was* sick.

My brother *feels* better.

My brother *is* a damn pizza eater.

By lunch I was having real trouble keeping my head in the game, trying hard not to smash everything in sight. Last period—advanced pea plants—I kept my head down and tried to distract myself by pretending to count pollinated flower heads. It didn't help. I couldn't stop thinking. Pure rage roared in my head.

Last January when Tom's liver shut down temporarily because of the chemotherapy and everybody started crying, I was okay. I knew, I KNEW, Tom was going to get better. I had faith. I prayed all the time. I believed.

After every medical setback, I just worked harder. I made my bed and nagged the little kids until they actually brushed their teeth before school. I helped Ashley fix her hair while Kelsey made sack lunches and Dad checked homework before he called the hospital for the daily morning bad-news bulletin about Tom. I paid attention at school, mostly, even during Mrs. Patten's deeply boring social studies class, because I knew God was looking down, checking it out, making sure I was holding up my end of the deal. Making sure I did everything right. And I did. Right? Because Tom was getting better. Finally getting better.

This morning Mom had walked around with a relieved smile, humming into her toast. She hadn't smoked one cigarette. During her big chat with Dad I caught another news bulletin. Tom's immune system was so strong that his oncologist had declared the bronchitis quarantine over. Dad and Kelsey and the little kids were coming up that weekend; everything was good, really fine—great, even. The last treatment. Tom was going to be done with cancer.

Everybody was fine about everything. Everybody but me. Suddenly, all I wanted to do was get even with him for all of this. For all of it, but especially for January tenth.

January tenth, the third day of no liver function, Tom as yellow and leathery as an old boot. Me and Grandma and all the relatives squeezed into the intensive care unit's family waiting room. Right next to the chapel at the hospital. And we were all being loud and cheerful and normal, the aunts talking a mile a minute while the uncles watched OSU make good against Michigan in double overtime. Ashley and Dylan and a bunch of cousins thundered in and out of the room. Kelsey made a million phone calls recruiting her friends into the decorating committee for a school dance. I sat next to Grandma on a couch, half reading a magazine, half watching the game.

I don't think Grandma had said two words all morning. Just stared at the backs of her old hands like she'd never seen such interesting wrinkles before. Then she stood up. "I'm too old for this," she said. "And I'm done with it." She brushed down the back of her dress. "John, take me home, now."

Uncle John turned from the group bunched in front of the TV, surprised. "You want to go home now?"

"Go home?" echoed Aunt Mary from the group bunched around the table at the other end of the room. "Don't you want to be here, Mom? When things change? You'll feel better if you stay here till things change. One of them medicines is bound to kick in any time."

Grandma gave her a long look. "Medicine ain't gonna do him a bit of good."

Aunt Mary just sat there, mouth open, like Grandma had conked her over the head with one of the waiting-room chairs. Every single Bainter in the room went quiet at the same time, trying real hard not to look at each other. Unbelievable, watching Grandma pick up her pocketbook and walk out of that silent waiting room. January tenth, yep yep. I'll never forget it as long as I live. That's my birthday. I turned thirteen years old in that stupid ICU waiting room, reading a year-old magazine and watching Grandma give up on Tom.

So I was thinking back to my birthday, trying to remember if I ever did get any presents. And I was thinking hard about getting even, thinking so hard that I had to hustle back to the biology lab after I changed into my ball uniform. I had left my glove in the pea plants.

In the dugout Mrs. Pangbourn gave me the fisheye for being late and put me at number six bat against Amesville. I shrugged and ignored her. Jeez. Any farther down the list and I'd be batting relief for the equipment manager.

I grabbed my glove and got out of there fast. Turned toward the Amesville dugout and about got run over by the little surprise Mom had mentioned just that morning.

"The guys made me the Amesville batboy!" shrieked Dylan, charging over and barreling into my legs. "On a unynimous vote! I been to all the games! I made Mommy promise not to tell! Because I wanted to surprise you!"

He hugged me hard. "Are you surprised?"

Man. Part of me was so happy to see him, I swear, I couldn't stop grinning. "Whoa, you're the batboy, huh? Pretty important stuff."

I picked him up and looked him eye to eye, real serious. "So if you're the best bat, then where're your sunflower seeds, pal? You hiding them in your back pockets?" I turned him upside down and shook him by his legs. Dylan squealed in delight as his cap fell off, feathery hair bouncing in the sunlight like a goofy wrong-side-up dandelion.

"Whoa, did I just shake a fart loose? Pee-yew, Dylan."

I set him right side up and punched him between his shoulder blades in sheer happiness. He looked at me, eyes shining.

"I missed you so much," he said. "I can't wait to see you hit."

My grin faded. The part of me that was living and breathing and eating with this stupid slump was beyond chopped. Great, so now I get to fail in front of Dylan, too? Was this it—big brothers slump, or get sick, or run off and get married, or one pointless thing after another while the little brothers hang around and watch, maybe try to pick up the pieces?

Fortunately, Ross trotted over in his catcher's gear just then. Dylan hung on to my shirt as we threw a little bit in front of the Upper West dugout.

"Are they batting you at three or four?" Ross asked.

I threw the ball back. "Six," I said, like it didn't make a bit of difference.

"Six?! Oh, man!" Ross looked worriedly over at the Upper West dugout as he threw. "What, they got some ball hitters we've never seen?"

"Nah, I'm slumping."

Dylan patted my leg. "Slumping, huh? That don't matter now. Because I'm here to back you up. You'll hit 'em a mile. You'll see."

"Yo, Buzz Bomb," Ross said to Dylan. "Remember what we talked about? How Matt is on the enemy team and we gotta whip his butt?"

"Sure. I remember." Dylan looked up at me and whispered, "But I'm still gonna root for you, Matt. In secret. Don't tell the guys."

I pulled his cap down over his eyes. Ross, on the other hand, was not going to be rooting for me anytime soon. "Hey, great, Matt. Slumping. I know what outfielder I'm hitting to."

"Go right ahead," I said, popping the ball out of my

glove and firing it into Ross's mitt. "The glove is as good as ever." Ross grinned.

Tyler and a couple other Amesville guys wandered over to tell me how great the team was doing without me. "Though the number of female fans has dropped to like none," observed Andy Lehman, the shortstop. "'Cause they can't sit behind the outfield fence and yell 'Maaaath-yew! Yoo-hoo! Mattie!' and make kissy noises."

"Hey, Matt?" said Dylan. "For real do you want some sunflower seeds? Because we got lots. I left 'em right there." He pointed to the Amesville dugout. Todd Striker, human lard bucket and my replacement in center field, smirked at me. He was eating a candy bar. A huge Wal-Mart bag full of sunflower seed packs overflowed beside him on the bench.

"Won't be nothing left by third inning," observed Ross. "Maybe we shoulda taken Coach up on the Ashley Bradshaw thing."

We broke up a couple of minutes later, the Amesville guys heading for their dugout. Ross stayed behind. He opened his mouth to say something. I cut him off.

"Don't start nothing with me," I warned. "I'm thinking about the game."

He shook his head, then turned toward the dugout. "Okay. Then we're gonna have a talk after," he said over his shoulder.

"Yeah. After," I murmured.

Alone, I bounced up and down in front of the Upper West dugout. "You gotta get ready, you gotta get ready," I muttered—then said it louder. Once I said it, it felt so good. I faded back into the dugout, still bouncing, the Upper West players talking, horsing around a little, putting on gloves and caps.

"Hey, Matt, you're gonna hit today; I can feel it," called the left fielder, but I was already out of there, jogging out to center field like I didn't have a thing on my mind but winning that ball game.

Short center right, I set up. Dug my spikes into the grass and pivoted left, then right. Grass was dry and short. The ball was gonna do some rolling today. I squinted up at the sun, the sky, looked up at the cracks shaped like an alligator.

*"No. He stays,"* said Tom's drugged-out voice in center field. *"Mom? Dad? Matt stays. Knows what's going on."*

*"Okay,"* said Dad's voice after a minute. *"Matt can stay."*

Shaun Mayle stepped into the box. Lefty Shaun's favorite hit was a long blast into right field. I bounced up on the balls of my feet and yelled at the right fielder to "Get ready yep yep."

*"Well."* The oncologist fiddled with Tom's medical chart, rustling the pages in my ear. *"A bone marrow transplant is certainly worth a try. You're a good candidate, Tom. You're young and otherwise healthy. But I'm telling*

*you and your family that a marrow transplant is not a sure thing."*

Shaun let a couple of pitches go by. I broke into a cold sweat just looking at him. Watching for him. Waiting for him. Stuff happened so fast.

Shaun swung.

The oncologist cleared his throat. *"It's the treatment of last resort."*

Wonder of wonders, Shaun popped it up into the first-base glove. A mighty nice chorus of "Yep yep yeps" called and echoed across the field. I pulled my cap down over my eyes. One down.

*"Treatment of last resort?"* echoed Tom's voice faintly. *"Sounds bad. Last treatment. Better."*

"Don't be stupid, Tom," I said as the next batter swung, and the ball gonged hollowly against the bat. My voice sounded so strange to me—scratchy, like a bad recording. "Don't matter. Either way you get better." The ball went up, lost in the sun, swallowed by the alligator as the crowd roared, and I ran it flat out.

Tom sighed. *"You really believe that, Matt?"*

I wasn't fast enough. The ball dropped deep left center. The game was on.

I had never played on a team facing Amesville Middle School before, and I hope I never have to again. They are tough. Unbelievably quick base runners. They loaded the bases twice in the first inning and scored four of those as runs, mainly by blowing past Upper West's catcher while he was still stepping up for the ball. On the third out, the poor guy stumbled into the dugout, covered in dirt and sweating bullets.

Coach Pangbourn stuck her finger under his nose. "I told you all season your short throws to second were gonna get you in trouble. They're gonna run you on every pitch unless you start throwing that ball."

I walked over to Upper West's leadoff batter. "See that guy in center field?" I said. "His name is Todd Striker. He cannot catch. He cannot throw."

The leadoff looked at me and grinned. "That so?"

I nodded. "It's got to be a long ball, though. You drop it anywhere near second base, and Zach out there will be happy to stuff it back down your throat."

Coach grabbed my arm. "Coach first base, Matt. You know how to read Amesville's catcher." She raised her voice. "Listen up. You run when Matt says run. You stick when Matt says stick. Period."

"Hey, Matt," said Lucas Brown as I set up in the coaching box at first. "How's your brother?"

"Doing good," I said absently. Upper West's batter took two pitches, then uncorked a beautiful hit, deep center. Todd lumbered after it.

"Uh-huh. Guess you told 'em about our little problem in center field," observed Luke as Upper West's batter slid into third. I shrugged.

It was a pretty good inning. I caught Ross holding a pitch just long enough to send Upper West's extremely fast three bat careening into second base. Ross shook his glove at me and scowled. I grinned. I could definitely get to like this coaching stuff.

The inning ended, and Upper West scored three. Barely.

"Shut 'em down, shut 'em down!" bellowed Coach as Upper West took the field. "Defense wins ball games!"

The catcher took Coach's comments to heart. He started throwing like he meant it. Amesville went down, fighting hard, with no score. In the dugout, Coach Pangbourn's grin turned wolfish.

"Well, gentlemen, I believe we have a real ball game going on here." She tossed me a batting helmet. "Go, Matt. Get a hit."

No doubt I was totally ready to get a hit, but the bat had other plans. I banged Tyler's first pitch into the Amesville dugout.

"Yoo-hoo! Left field's behind me, Matt, sweetie!" yelled Andy.

"That was one ugly hit, Matt," said Ross, as I toed back in the batter's box and lifted my hand-poured, custom-made titanium dead fish. "You kinda got me hoping you'll hit one."

I struck out. Tyler shrugged in sympathy.

Amesville managed to cut loose a little in the third,

which brought the score up seven to three. Upper West crept back in the fourth, after I popped up straight into Todd Striker's glove. Good old Todd. He stood stock-still out there in center field, admiring the unusual sight of a real live baseball in his glove. The runner on third tagged up and went home.

"Wake up, Todd!" Andy yelled. The runner at second was stealing third. Todd threw the ball into foul-territory dirt about four feet beyond Andy's glove. The runner rounded third and dove for home. Seven to five.

I closed my eyes against the pain. Sure, I was happy to help the team out like that, but jeez. Once Todd Striker starts catching what comes off your bat, it's time to stop playing ball.

Upper West clawed out another run in the fifth and managed to hold Amesville off, so by the top of the sixth inning, the score stood at seven to six. I was pretty fed up, standing in the outfield and listening to those voices leave off discussing the treatment of last resort and start carping about my lousy hitting.

*"You're turning your wrist again,"* said Tom in my right ear.

*"A wider stance,"* suggested Marianne in my left ear.

*"Honey, if Matt stands any wider, Amesville's gonna think he's a wishbone and snap his little legs in two."*

I ground my teeth together and crouched way, way down over my glove—out of advice range. Though

Tom followed me down, there on the grass of deep center field, down for one last word.

*"Come to me,"* he said softly, softly so that Marianne wouldn't overhear, which was insane thinking on his part, seeing how I was the one hearing voices, not her.

I straightened up and wiped the sweat out of my cap. Two outs now, runners on second and third. I bounced on the balls of my feet, totally ready, totally concentrated.

"Why? Why should I?"

The batter connected. I moved in blindly toward the fly ball.

"Give me one reason why I should do one more thing. Because I already said good-bye to my friends and gave up my spot on the team and came up here and did everything right, everything I was supposed to! I even did my freakin' HOMEWORK!" I roared out loud as the ball fell into my glove.

"Whoa," said the second baseman from a couple of feet away. "Take it easy. That's three outs."

I flipped the ball onto the pitcher's mound and trotted into the dugout.

"Because I have held up my end of the deal," I whispered. "I changed your sheets and mopped up the bathroom floor at three o'clock in the morning and pretended not to hear you cry when it hurt so bad and I prayed and I never gave up, and now what?"

I threw my glove on the bench and picked up a batting helmet and a bat and strolled out of the dugout into foul territory, taking almighty practice swings like I was thinking about nothing but the next hit.

"What? Now what?" I muttered as I swung my bat around the world at the manicured grass and the spacious dugout with its rolls of fresh grip tape and the shiny chain-link fence and Upper West's domed observatory and its satellite dishes and skylights. "Now nothing. I got nothing."

*"Well, I got something for you,"* said Tom good-naturedly as I walked away from his voice and toward the deck. *"I got something. Just you and me."*

Well, screw that. What I needed was a hit. I swung the bat again. One good hit, and everything would start to be okay.

I stood on deck and ran stuff through my head one more time. It was the bottom of the sixth, down by a run. I needed a hit. I needed a hit bad.

When I dug into the batter's box, I got a brilliant idea. This slump wasn't about a little wrist problem. No, what I realized as I moved in and brought the bat up and felt the weight of the world over my shoulder was that I'd just been rolling over and letting the pitcher grab the plate. See, this slump was all about control. Stupid of me to give up control.

So I choked up and stepped in real close. Quick hands

to throw a quick bat. I leaned in, and behind me I heard Ross moan, "Oh, man, Matt!"

Tyler just stood on the mound shaking his head at me, all disgusted.

"He's gonna dust you back," Ross warned.

Well, I was tired of being dusted back. Pushed into one lousy drawer and the top of a desk. Dusted out of third bat, covered with pea plant pollen and subject-verb-object-complimented to death. I was sick of it, sick of the whole deal. Letting cancer get the best of me like that.

I kicked up a little cloud of dust and leaned in closer. "He throws at my head, I get him," I muttered.

"Go, Matt. Get a hit!" chirped Dylan from the dugout.

"Shut UP, Dylan!" yelled Ross.

Tyler got mad, of course, and flamed one straight at my ear. I hit the dirt. And came up charging the mound.

I got to hand it to Upper West Bexley, all those guys whose names I never did learn—all those guys who I let down in a big way with my bat. Five seconds after I knocked Tyler to the ground and punched him in the mouth, Upper West's bench emptied. So did Amesville's. We had a major pileup right on the pitcher's mound.

With two entire teams flailing away right over our heads and the fans screaming and throwing candy wrappers and pop cans onto the field, Tyler and me got packed in kind of tight. We stopped fighting and put our arms up to protect our heads from flying elbows and knees and sort of waited it out. After a minute, Ross worked his head and shoulders down to our vicinity.

"What is your problem, Matthew?" moaned Ross.

"You're gonna get—oof!—thrown out of the game, charging the mound like that," observed Tyler.

Coach Pangbourn's spikes came into view as she waded into the fight, pulling guys up by their shirts and tossing them all over the infield. She worked her way down to the bottom of the pile, finally, and yanked me to my feet.

Dylan's face, paper white, popped up under her elbow. He clutched at me. "Uh-oh, Matt. You okay, Matt?"

"In my office, Mr. Bainter!" snarled Coach Pang-bourn.

She let go of the front of my shirt like it was made out of dog turds. She turned away and went around yelling "Break it up!" to the little clots of players still rolling around on the grass and throwing half-hearted punches.

Well, I shook Dylan's hands off my arms and walked toward the school. I walked through the players' entrance in the chain-link fence near the dugout and climbed the hill. I cut through the teachers' parking lot, where I broke into a trot, then a run, and kept going—

"Matt!" yelled Dylan. "Matt, where you going? Maaaaaatt!"

—past the gym door, around the building, off the school grounds; past all those mansions and three-car garages and perfect emerald lawns; no sidewalks, no people, just the sun shining down on all that empty silence.

I remembered I was wearing spikes and ran faster. I burst past a gate, rounded an ivy-draped corner, and burned up the business section, where the sidewalks began.

"Wait up, Matt!"

I turned around. Ross had run all that way behind me. He'd come so fast he still had on his shin guards. His chest protector and face mask were probably lying on top of some rich guy's azalea bushes. Somebody back at the fight had connected with his nose. It was still bleeding. He stumbled up, wheezing bad and wiping the blood and snot off his face with the front of his shirt.

"I have never run so fast in my life," he gasped. He bent over, and I pounded him helpfully on the back.

"So," he said, still breathing hard. "You got money?"

"For what?" I asked.

"For the bus," said Ross simply. "A bus around here goes to the hospital, don't it?"

Now Ross Berg is pure smart, perceptive in a way that makes him such a great and natural catcher. Ross stops every pitch cold. He defends home plate with a pair of cast-iron fists and a ferocious grin stretching behind his mask. Ross Berg spends the whole game facing the field, catching Tyler's sixty-five-mile-an-hour fastballs and watching over his players—knowing down to his bones what's going on.

So Ross didn't have to spend but five minutes in the game before he knew. This was nothing about pea plants, or Upper West Bexley's championship run, or even about batting a putrid .193. This was about torture. Five minutes more and Ross knew. Forget my brother. This was about me. I was dying by inches.

I got on that bus shaking like a leaf. Everything was not great. Everything was not fine. Everything was silent and strange and scary. I couldn't fold my hands. I couldn't bow my head. I couldn't find the words.

Ross sat down next to me. He stayed real quiet, snuffling a little from the blood in his nose. Two dirty, bad-smelling, sweating kids in baseball uniforms. Nobody sat close to us.

# 10

## TUNNELS OF DARKNESS

**CHILDREN'S** Memorial was a series of huge steel and glass skyscrapers connected by third-floor skywalks. It sprawled next to the elegant City Center smack in downtown Columbus. Looking around at the folks brushing past, I realized you were supposed to wear mink coats and fine leather shoes to hang around this particular street corner. In our dirty ball uniforms, Ross and I looked like some kind of bug life.

We stopped in front of the hospital's revolving glass doors.

"How are we going to work this?" asked Ross.

We peered through the swish of the paddle doors at a cool chrome-and-green marble entrance. At one end of the lobby, a two-story waterfall thundered dramatically over the rocks into a goldfish pond. Across from the pond was the Patient Information Booth. Three hospital volunteers bused in from the toughest, meanest senior home in central Ohio lounged around, waiting to direct visitors to X-ray and boot dirty underage kids out of the hospital.

"Well," I said. "We go in and act like we own the place."

I pushed into the first empty wedge of the revolving doors. My spikes clickity-clacked merrily over the marble. Ross followed in the slice right behind me. But I didn't slide out into the lobby. Instead, I pushed all the way around and popped out again on the sidewalk. Ross popped out behind me. A lady in a furry coat gave us a dirty look.

"I got a better idea," I said.

We turned up a narrow cutback alley that ran between two buildings. We wandered around in the shadows cast by the skywalks far over our heads. From long experience with my mom, I knew we'd eventually find a little group of people huddled in front of a fire door, hunched over their cigarettes, puffing away. Sure enough, there they were. A coffee can full of butts propped open the fire door.

"We use the smokers' entrance. Easy," I said as I dodged the clouds of smoke and held open the door for Ross. "He's on the ninth floor."

We climbed a couple of flights of stairs, nobody climbing but us.

"So you been here a lot, huh?" puffed Ross.

"Nope."

"Oh. So you been here a couple of times? On Sundays or something, huh?"

"Nope."

Ross pulled me to a stop. "You been here one time before, definitely, right?"

I shook my head.

"Oh, man, Matt! I know you—you're gonna just walk in there like everything's a hundred percent okay, I'm so happy to see ya! Jeez! He's been on drugs and chemotherapy and who knows what crap! You gotta think about this!"

I jerked my arm free and kept climbing. "I'm done thinking," I muttered. Ross ran up the stairs and blocked my way.

"He still had hair, a little. Is he bald?"

I shrugged.

"Did the bone thing work?"

I shrugged again.

"Is he still dying?"

I shoved Ross into the wall hard with both hands and leaped past him. "He moved into the step-down unit!" I shouted. "He's doing that good."

We busted through the ninth-floor fire door together and careened to a stop at the beginning of a long hallway. Mom was right. This was a real nice hospital, more like a fancy hotel than any hospital I had ever seen. Calming pictures of flowers. Deep pile carpet. Tinkly

**121**

piano music over the intercom system. The whole hall-way was an ocean of soothing greys and greens—except for the tidal wave of pure white nurses thundering toward us from the other end of the hall at a dead run.

"Oh, man, Ross!"

Ross shoved me into a utility closet to the left of the fire door. "Wait here while I draw 'em off," he whispered and shut the door.

"You! Dirty little boy!" yelled a nurse. "This floor is restricted! What are you doing here?"

I opened the door a crack. Ross stumbled forward and held his left hand—his catcher's mitt hand—up in front of his face. It was a grim sight. His thick, callused palm was black and blue and swollen with broken blood vessels that came after a season of catching Tyler's fastball. His index and middle fingers have been jammed so many times, the doctor at the Amesville clin-ic got sick of taping Ross up after every game, so he showed Ross how to splint them at home.

Ross dropped his mitt hand and clutched dramati-cally at his throat. Two years ago, Ross got clipped by a foul ball that drove his throat guard into the soft, fleshy part on the side of his neck. The stitches left a raised red scar. When Ross turns his neck, the cartilage in his throat makes that scar stand way, way out. Looks exactly like Ross has just swallowed a chicken bone. Sideways.

That close-up look at Ross's mitt hand wrapped tightly around his chicken-bone neck made ten battle-hardened nurses screech to a stop.

"Argle bargle!" gasped Ross.

"Good grief, the kid's choking!" exclaimed a nurse.

"Punctured trachea," said another nurse crisply. "Look at the blood on his shirt."

The nurses wrestled Ross to the carpet. He rolled furiously, coughing and gasping, "Argle bargle!" while they tried to pin him down and apply emergency first aid. One nurse jumped up and beat it to the call desk, stat.

I eased out of the closet, hustled through an open door down the hallway, and closed it behind me. Ross was my true friend. I just hoped those nurses didn't hurt him too bad when they found out he was perfectly healthy.

"Hello," said a quavery voice.

I turned around. In the bed was an enormously fat old lady. She looked at me steadily.

"Hello," she said again. Hey, maybe Tom wouldn't be bald, because this lady sure had hair, lots of it, shining blue in the brilliant afternoon sun pouring through a gap in the curtains.

"Hello," I whispered. "I'll leave in a minute. When all the commotion in the hallway settles down. Okay?"

"You're my first baseball player."

"Ma'am?"

"Oh, yes, my first ballplayer. So far I've been visited by tunnels of darkness, voices of light, a couple of angels, and my old collie dog, Velvet. The Lord Himself came yesterday. We had a nice visit. But you're my first ballplayer." A slight frown crossed her face. "I never learned how to play myself. Never had the time."

"Well, ma'am, it's a great team sport." With that many visitations, she had obviously been here a while, so I asked her, "Do you know what room Thomas Bainter is in?"

She lifted her head a little. "Thomas Bainter? Did he play for the Indians?"

"Oh, no, ma'am, he—"

"You're not here to point out how I failed to keep up with sports in my life, are you? Now, you celestial beings ought to remember how I had the three kids to raise all by myself after Ed was killed in Korea."

"Uh, ma'am—"

"And when Uncle Buster needed a place to stay after his operation, I didn't hesitate a minute. 'Come on home with me, Uncle Buster,' I told him. 'I'll take care of you for as long as you got.' The man lived another seventeen years! Buried him on Columbus Day, 1973. So don't tell me, young man, I missed the boat by not spending more time playing baseball!"

"I think you—"

124

Her head thumped back on the pillow. "I shouldn't be reproached at the end of my life with my lack of athletic skills," she said, sniffing. "You can't do everything, you know. Besides, I was a darned good dancer."

I gave up, dodged across the hall, and talked through the oxygen tent of a man from Chauncey, who'd heard there was a boy from Amesville in the step-down rooms down the hall and on the left.

## 11

## VOICES OF LIGHT

**TOM** sat in the middle of his bed in the middle of the room in the middle of a patch of sunlight, reading a fat paperback with a picture of colliding planets on the cover. He was also in the middle of a blood transfusion. An IV pole had a sack of blood taped to it. A tube ran along his ankle and disappeared up the leg of his gray sweat pants. The sack of blood glowed in the sun. The tube was a ruby wire. Tom looked up and smiled at me.

He wasn't much more than a bag of bones dressed up for Halloween. Sure enough, he had lost all his hair—eyebrows, eyelashes, the fine hair on his arms, on his toes—everything. Smooth and shiny, his cheeks rosy from the transfusion, he glowed a little, too, like an empty snail shell held up between your eye and the sun on a hot summer day.

"'Bout time you got here," he said. He stuck his finger in the book to mark his place, like he knew that he'd get a chance to finish it before anybody let him check out of the hospital. He was having trouble holding the covers shut. "You missed all the scary parts."

"I don't know about that," I said. "My heart's beating pretty fast, looking at you like this." I moved a little closer. "Sorry I'm so dirty."

"Hey, my blood counts are way up there. They gave me back my toothbrush last night." He ran his tongue pleasurably around his mouth. "My mouth sores are gone, about. I can tolerate a little raw dirt."

Trembling, I dropped onto the brown vinyl sofa. I hadn't cried once that past year. Suddenly, I was close to it. Looking at my brother like that, all burned out and hairless and smiling faintly at me.

"Mom left a couple of minutes ago," Tom said. "She got a call from your school. Something about a fight."

I waved my hand, blowing off the fight. "That was nothing. Just Tyler Smith being a jerk. You know."

I leaned back, pulled my cap down a little. "You know what Mom and Dad got me for my birthday this year?"

He shook his head. "Nah. Never heard. Was it something good?"

I stared, slit-eyed, at him for a minute. Then I settled my cap a little lower, so he wouldn't see the truth on my face. Honest, I didn't want him to see. I wasn't gonna say anything. I'd gotten so good at not saying anything. But it leaked out anyway. Like something inside had busted for good.

"I hate you," I muttered, "for sucking up my life. Liver failure on my birthday, thank you so much. I come up here to back you up and you don't care; you leave me and go off and get married. Don't need you so much anymore, Matt, ol' pal, so stop trying so hard and give it a rest and hit crap for a fourth-place crap team. That's the deal."

Not everything was wonderful about this hospital. I rubbed my shoulders against the hard brown vinyl and settled deeper into the lumpy cushions. "What am I doing up here, even? Being tough. Being brave. For what?"

Weird. It took me by surprise, a little. Feeling stuff I never thought I could feel, not in a million years. I hated him. I hated him. And yeah, maybe for a split second I wished he'd just get it over with already, so I could be sad, and remember him with fondness, and carry on his memory, and get back to my freaking *life* instead of this endless, endless waiting. "Aw, screw it, Tom. You wouldn't understand."

"Bet you fifty bucks I know what you're thinking." His voice all quiet and bitter. Just ripped right out of him. "You're thinking, man, I wish he'd get it over with."

Believe me, that made me sit a little straighter.

"Because," he said, examining the ceiling tiles over my head, "because I think the same thing. Man. Just get it over with, eh? But I can't. I got to try. I don't even know why anymore. Just keep going."

His voice. Just the one voice, murmuring. "It's stupid to hate you, Matt. But I do. I don't want to, but I do. You're the healthy one. You're gonna live happily ever after."

He must have found his favorite tile, because he stared up there for a long time, silent. He'd run out of things to say. So had I. That was a good thing, because with so much truth circulating, it was already pretty hard to breathe the air in the room. Any more, and we'd have to weep. Or fight. Or both.

So we both stayed quiet. And after a little while of silence, the adrenaline wore off. And the trembling, tearing anger wore off. Suddenly, all I wanted to do was sleep. I closed both eyes and yawned.

"Happily ever after, huh?" I mumbled. "Okay, deal. Right after my nap and something major to eat."

Tom snorted. "Sure, Matt. No problem. We'll get the aide to mix up a couple of soymilks."

I cracked open one eye, amused. "Bet she won't put in extra cinnamon like I do."

Tom shook his head. "You never give up, do you?"

"Yeah, actually, I do. I give up." I closed my eyes and drowsed a little. I listened to Tom turn the pages of his book.

"I've been thinking about home," Tom said after a

couple of minutes. "I've been thinking about Marianne. She comes up every Saturday after work and stays with me till Sunday night. Sleeps right on that sofa. It's a long drive for that Chevy of hers."

He moved his legs restlessly, and the sack of blood rubbed gently against the pole. "She couldn't make it last weekend. I miss her."

"Ummm," I said dreamily. I was back in center field, hearing Tom murmur in my ear.

"I'm ready," he said. "I'm ready to go home. I know I am. And today's Friday. If I went home now, I could save Marianne the trip—"

Slowly I opened one eye. "Huh?"

"—you could help me. Now that you're finally here. You get me on the bus for home. Surprise Marianne."

I sat up so fast the ball cap fell off my head. "You want to go home?"

I looked at my brother, nineteen years old and shrunk back down to my size, head shining like a raw egg in that patch of sunlight.

"I've been here long enough," he said distinctly in my ears, both of them, from across the room. "I've done everything they said to. All the rest is just wait and see."

"Well," I said slowly, thinking. One more thing, but I could do it. Get him out the door, we'd go home, Tom would be set. If I got Tom home in one piece, I could be done. My heart beat a little faster. "Well, if we busted in okay, I guess we can bust back out." I rotated my wrists and grinned.

Tom's gray sweats looked pretty much like my dirty baseball uniform. We put the Upper West Bexley cap on Tom's skull. It sank down a little and rested on his ears so you didn't notice about his eyebrows unless you peered into the shadow of the cap, and who would do that? Tom turned off the IV and disconnected the tube at his ankle.

"The rest of the tube runs up to a vein in my thigh," he explained as he eased his bony feet into the sneakers I had found in the closet. "They had to close my port. The nurses tell me the only good veins I got left are the ones running up my crotch."

I winced. "Jeez, Tom." I helped him to his feet. I swear to you, he was rock steady. Standing there strong and upright.

We strolled down the hallway, not a soul in sight. It was just like how Tom would wait for me after a game. Marianne would walk to the parking lot talking with Mom and Kelsey, the little kids would race ahead and fight over who had to sit in the middle of the backseat, but Tom would hang around the dugout and wait for me. Walk me back to the van. We didn't talk much. We didn't have to.

The elevator doors opened the second Tom touched the DOWN button. We stepped in and turned around as the doors closed. Two kid ballplayers. Observing the end of visiting hours.

We walked past the waterfall, past the Patient Information Booth, past the Security Office. The office door was open partway. A security guy sat behind the desk, head down, shuffling papers, trying not to giggle. Ross stood in front of the desk, on the phone, getting chewed out by his dad. I could hear Mr. Berg's voice clear through the receiver as we crossed the lobby.

Ross watched us walk by. He waved wistfully, then snatched the cap off his head and tossed it through the door.

I put Ross's cap on my head. It was great—amazingly great—being under the faded red *A* again. Tom and I strolled through the lobby and straight out the revolving doors. Two kid ballplayers. On their way home.

A southbound bus stood right outside, doors open, waiting for us. That was the kind of day it was. A great day—no, a miraculous day. One pitch, and I could have knocked the ball straight through a window on the ninth floor of Children's Memorial. My batting slump was definitely over.

# 12

## GHOST RUNNER

**WE** sat down on the driver's side of the bus toward the back.

"Whoa," said Tom, "it's bright out here." He blinked three or four times. "I can hardly see."

He put his pale hand around the metal grip on the seat in front of us. His wedding ring, a size too big, clinked against the metal. "Two months shut away inside with the overhead light on night and day. I feel like a ghost let off his chain."

He turned eagerly to the window. "Lookit there. There's cars and people, and the sun's blazing hot on the window." He touched the gritty window with his fingers before he turned back to me. "And frankly, Matt, you stink."

"Well, I had to play baseball and get into a fight and bust you out of the hospital today," I said. "I've been too busy to drop everything and take a shower." Tom grinned and turned back to the window.

I looked around a little. The bus was almost empty. Weird. Here in the heart of downtown Columbus you'd think more people would need to go south. More than just Tom and me and an old man sitting in the back of the bus on the other side of the aisle.

But the doors closed, and the bus took off with just us three. Tom was all over that window like a kid, pressing his nose against the glass, yelling out stuff over the diesel whine of the bus engine.

"Lookit! A Pizza Barn!"

"Yeah!" I yelled back.

"Makes me hungry!"

"Yeah!"

"Hey, that guy just jaywalked!"

"Yeah!"

"Hey, he's jaywalking into the Pizza Barn! Man, oh man, oh man, that's what I call living it up!"

"Yeah!"

I started to snicker. I couldn't help it. I was speechless with joy, lighter than air, a thousand feet off the ground, sailing up and over the chain-link fence, dropping down beyond the pea plants and eighteen-room mansions and outfields where I didn't belong, dropping outside the bone cancer fence. Taking care of my brother, hitting him around the bases. Getting him where he'd be safe. Home.

"This is smart," said Tom quietly, staring out the window. I could barely make out the words. "This is the way to do it. Go home and surprise Marianne. I got to go home and be with her." He leaned his head against the window and watched the shabby apartment buildings roll by, one after another. A faint smile sat on his lips.

Tom didn't talk anymore. So I shut up and lounged in my seat next to him. The bus idled along in traffic, not really going much of anywhere. A hot, peaceful bus ride, sunset pouring in the windows. I was thinking maybe we'd get home in time for a large snack before bedtime. I was starving. Dog tired. So I was thinking about that, thinking how I needed to get home right then about as much as Tom ever did. Then the old guy behind us changed everything. He started to cry.

I couldn't believe it. I glanced back, furious that somebody could cry in the face of all our Bainter happiness. Such an average old guy, too—comb marks through his silver hair; battered hat; beat-up wooden cane hooked on the seat in front of him, its tip worn by tapping out miles of sidewalks—a guy like that ought to know better than to lose it in public. But he was floating away on a river of sorrow, weeping it all into a snow-white handkerchief so big it hung down to his knees and covered his face. I couldn't catch his eye, stare him down. Make him stop it. Cut it out right there, pal; all that sorrow and grief you'd think somebody had just—

I turned around and faced the front alongside my brother. I concentrated on the pure joy we had shared watching the jaywalker, but it wasn't much use. Rage like acid flooded the back of my throat.

Cancer ought to take out feeble old guys like that crier. He was no good to anybody anymore. But Tom. Tom. My hands clenched into knuckleball fists as I leaned my elbows against my knees, and oh God, how I prayed to regain the shining arc of trajectory over the chain-link fence, back, back, back, the runner trotting safe toward home . . .

Well. That hit me like a hand-poured, custom-made titanium bat upside the head. Home.

"Tom?" I spoke up. "Where we going?"

Or maybe I didn't say anything, I don't know. Maybe it was just another voice muttering on and on whether I wanted to hear it or not.

Where we going? Back to the kid-packed, germ-jungle Bainter house, so the next round of head colds could wipe out Tom's immune system and send him back to critical care? 'Course, he's married now, so maybe the bus could drop him off at Marianne's one-room apartment over the service bays of the Amesville Gas 'n' Save. Now *that* would be really healthy for a guy whose liver was already damaged from twenty different toxic chemicals injected, radiated, swallowed, and inhaled for his own damn good over the last six months.

Where we going? Trembling, I pulled Ross's ball cap lower on my forehead. There was no safe. There was no home. We were adrift, Tom and me, on account of a tumor no bigger than the pencil eraser I had used on all those crappy English essays. Nothing was safe. Nowhere was home.

The bus rolled slowly south and a little west in heavy afternoon traffic. It wouldn't matter how far we rode. The truth rode along with us. The truth was, I didn't hate Tom. The truth was, I'd do anything for him. Anything. I'd give up baseball. Never again touch a bat, never throw a ball, never feel the roll of dirt under my spikes as I ran the bases—I'd never look back, not once. I'd grab a deal like that with both hands. Trade baseball for my brother? Absolutely.

But there were no deals. Never had been. There was only this bus ride. And after this bus ride—after everything that had gone on before it and everything that would go on after it—my brother still might die of bone cancer.

The old guy behind us folded up his handkerchief and pulled the stop cord. The bus swung over to the curb. Blinding light from the setting sun poured through the windshield. It filled the bus and made it impossible to see. The old man unhooked his cane and tottered up the aisle, walking straight into that blinding light.

He came up beside me. He stumbled a bit and put out his hand for the handgrip on the back of my seat but came up with my shoulder instead. His hand—huge, warm, steady, alive—rested. And I heard him say in a quiet voice:

*"One more thing"*

but maybe I didn't. Maybe he didn't say a single word, just let his hand rest on my shoulder, my hand holding his where I had reached up to steady him, where I had grabbed his hand in hope and fear and dread and gratefulness as the bus swayed and glowed. Next to me, Tom sighed.

The old man fumbled with his cane. He let go of my shoulder, then walked down the aisle of light and out the door.

And Tom and me rode the bus to the end of the line on a big old boulevard called Refugee Road. We got out at a used-car lot and a bingo hall and a boarded-up movie theater.

Oh, and the bus depot. Right across from us on that wide and empty street.

Tom collapsed onto the bus-stop bench, listing slightly to the left. I sat down next to him. All the hilarity, all the joy, all the longing for home had leaked out of him like a toy balloon. We just sat there, looking nowhere in particular, while the white evening sky pressed down on our heads.

The wind blew a crumpled newspaper against his leg. I bent over to push it away. His IV tube had leaked a watery red line of blood and platelets down his shin, wetting his shoe. The world was silent, except for the wind and a long, high siren still miles away, coming toward us.

"Tom?" I whispered. "You gonna make it?"

He closed his eyes and put his head on my shoulder. "Yeah, yeah. Give it a rest, Mommy," he said and slumped against me.

We sat there, not two hundred yards from the bus for home. Two hundred lousy yards, where it all fell to pieces, finally. Tom slumped against me while tears burned slowly down my cheeks, and the siren got closer and closer.

The ambulance pulled up. Mom got out from the passenger-side door. "No, it's them. We found them," she said into the Harrisons' cell phone. "Yeah. The bus for home, like I thought." She turned it off and sat down next to me.

The EMTs opened the swing doors under the flashing lights, unfolded the stretcher, and locked the wheels in place. Mom's arm pressed in hot and twitchy on my left. I felt Tom's bone-thin elbow, cold and weightless, on my right.

After a while Mom sighed and handed me half of her soggy wad of tissues. "Jesus God Almighty Father in Heaven," she murmured.

I listened carefully. It wasn't cussing. It was prayer.

# 13

## HOLDING AT THIRD

**THE** ambulance took Tom back to Children's Memorial, back to his room with a view of the ninth-floor nurses' station. He spent the next twenty-four hours in a sterile, laminar air-flow room while the nurses scurried around, and the doctors glared at me like I was a criminal. Though Mom had a different way of looking at it.

"Wish I'd thought of it," she said in the hallway when she brought Dylan by to say good night. "Busting him out like that. Pure genius."

Dylan looked me over. "Todd Striker didn't even leave the dugout during the fight. He just sat there saying you were gonna get thrown out of the game. What a weenie."

I picked him up and looked him eye to eye. "Not like you. You were right out there, backing me up. I appreciate it."

"Yeah," he said, hugging my neck. I hugged him

back. "But I didn't hit anybody. Mommy would get mad."

"Yep, Mommy sure would," said Mom. "Real mad, real fast. C'mon, kiddo. Say good night to Matt. It's late. Let's hit the road."

Dylan frowned. "Nah, I'm staying here. With Matt." His fingers monkey-gripped my shirt.

I turned his head with my hand and looked him over. "Yeah? Then who'll bring me breakfast in the morning? I bet you fifty bucks you don't know what kind of Egg McMuffin I like best."

Dylan stuck out his jaw. "You think? Extra cheese. Pay up."

I refused to leave. All evening I strolled up and down in the corridor outside Tom's room saying "Hiya" to the nurses and phlebotomists and oncologists until the night nurse finally took me into an empty room and told me to shower off head to toe with antiseptic soap. She gave me a pair of gray sweats and paper slippers and a surgical mask to cover my nose and mouth. With wet hair and antiseptic soap still in my ears, I looked like a drowned-rat cancer patient myself. We ducked into Tom's room.

"I have a little brother," she said to me in a low voice. "He's a pain in the neck, too." She nodded toward the bed. "You're on bedpan duty till seven A.M."

I sat down on the sofa.

"We almost made it," said Tom after a while, from the middle of his bed in the middle of the dark.

I pulled down the surgical mask. "Five minutes more."

"Man oh man oh man, couldn't you just see everybody's faces eating dust as we waved bye-yah from the back of the bus to Amesville?"

"Catch you later . . ."

". . . See you around . . ."

"Yeah."

"Yeah. Five minutes more," he said. "But. This is how it worked out, huh?" He took a breath, and then another. "Just one more thing. I've been saying that a lot lately."

The last voice drifted through the room, rustling at the curtains, fanning up the small hairs on the back of my neck. *One more thing.*

My fingers folded, one into the other. My eyes drifted shut. *"Okay,"* I told him. *"Whatever happens . . . okay."*

*"Atta boy, Matt."*

"Matt?"

"Yeah?"

"Could you find somebody? I have a headache. I need an aspirin or something."

Tom developed a low-grade fever. It took him a week to shake it. But the fever broke, his white-cell count remained low-normal, and his oncologist couldn't cook up another reason to keep him. So Tom was being discharged from Children's Memorial. And we were going home.

It didn't take a lot of time to pack the stuff I had brought with me to Upper West Bexley. After all, I only had the top of the desk and one bureau drawer to clear. I reached into the drawer and felt around. Something was stuck between the top drawer and the back of the bureau.

I yanked on the handles. The drawer fell out and whacked my leg. A pair of my socks dropped from the back of the drawer frame and onto a messy pile of Rickey Harrison's clothes jammed into the second drawer. I looked a little closer and about passed out. My socks lay nestled on a jumble of sports bras printed with crossed tennis rackets and pink basketball hoops.

"Rickey Harrison is a GIRL!" I yelled. I jumped away like those bras were killer bees.

Mom stopped in the open doorway, the laundry basket full of bathroom stuff in her hands. "You knew Rickey was a girl." She popped a bubble in her nicotine gum.

I stared into the new full-length mirror we had put up last night. My face was sicko gray. "I've been living in a girl's room," I whispered. "Sleeping in a girl's BED . . ."

"Well, you know Rickey Harrison."

"... No ..."

"Sure you do. You met her before they left for Africa. Remember? They visited our church, and she was this sweet little—"

"... No ..."

"And when the youth group played softball after the potluck, you said she had a great throwing arm—"

"... No ..."

"—for a girl."

"... No ... no nonono. Wait a minute. That was Rickey Harrison?"

I definitely remembered Rickey. Halfway through the game, her team down a couple runs, she got carried away and slid into second with her spike-foot aimed directly at the baseman's kneecap. If she hadn't taken off her church high heels to play barefoot, it would have been ugly. Okay, so she wasn't so bad. But, believe me, I left those socks right where they lay. I was not about to touch Rickey Harrison's ... stuff.

We drove over to Upper West Middle School to collect my crummy grades and say good-bye. Mrs. Pangbourn strode into her office, threw a manila folder on her desk, and sat down. Her gaze wandered over to my mom, then to me.

"No tie, huh?" she said.

"Nope. Guys from Amesville don't wear them much."

She looked me over, then grinned at Mom. "I'm pleased to meet you, Mrs. Bainter, if only to say good-bye." That sounded good, except Mrs. Pangbourn already met Mom, of course, the day of the fight. The day Tom and I tried to go home.

"It was a pleasure having Matt on the team," continued Mrs. Pangbourn. "Now that he's got his hitting back"—she raised an eyebrow at me—"I sure wish he could hang around and see us through to state."

I had to admit, a part of me wished I could, too. I was going home in time for playoffs. I just wasn't going to play. The Ohio Athletic Board declared me ineligible to join Amesville after playing the regular season with Upper West. My season was ending with a whopping .223. Pathetic, sure, but Upper West closed on a four-game winning streak.

"Tied for third." Mrs. Pangbourn rubbed her hands together and gloated. "Thanks, Matt."

"Happy to help," I said, lounging in my chair. Tied for third or not, Upper West wouldn't make it out of sectionals alive. Amesville, on the other hand, would definitely go to state. Their season's center fielder, Todd Striker, was getting the ride of his lard-bucket life. Atta boy, Todd.

"This must be a happy day for you," said Mrs. Pangbourn, looking at my mom. "Having your son out of the hospital, all of you going home."

I checked the clock on the wall. Right about now Marianne'd be pushing Tom in a wheelchair out the main entrance of Children's Memorial. She'd pop a little wheelie over the threshold and out to her loaner car, Reverend Lohse's 1984 Lincoln Continental, parked illegally in the bus zone. She'd hold her face up. "Don't that sun feel good, Tom? Just another real pretty day."

And Marianne would drive them back to Amesville, the sun on their faces, back to the Ten-Mile-High Nursing Home. Turned out I'd been right, wondering where Tom's home would be. Mom and the social worker had been discussing it, wondering what to do. But once my season ground to a halt, once I got my head out of the game and into the rest of my life, it was easy to figure out. I made a couple of phone calls to the Baptist Society. Sort of filled them in on the situation. Got a real nice answer, too—an answer big enough to pay for a step-down room at the Ten-Mile. A home for Tom. For as long as he needed it.

I rotated my wrists. Not bad for a guy who had been walking around the past couple of months with—let's face it—all the communication skills of a highly intelligent squid.

"Going home," repeated my mom, grinning. "We are going home."

"So. What's his prognosis?" asked Mrs. Pangbourn.

I hadn't spent the last two weeks reading everything

I could get my hands on about Ewing's sarcoma for nothing. Maybe I hadn't worn a tie, but there was more than one way to impress a principal. I toed down into the school's carpet and swung hard. Maximum wrist snap.

"Fifty-four to sixty-nine percent survival rate over five years," I said, "with a nonmetastatic tumor the size of Tom's. They threw everything they had at it—surgery, radiation, chemotherapy. A bone marrow transplant. The future's hard to see, you know? His liver function's already not so hot. Tom might suffer hearing loss, develop cataracts. He'll catch every single virus on the planet and turn them into pneumonia, probably. He and Marianne might not be able to have kids."

Mom slapped my hand. "Shame on you. Not hoping real hard for a nephew."

I shrugged. "Then again, the cancer might reoccur."

Mom took her hand away from mine and sighed. But Mrs. Pangbourn watched me steadily. "Matt?"

"Yeah?"

"You kept your eyes open the whole time. That's great."

"Yeah." I looked out the window, felt the sun on my face. "Whatever happens . . . it's gonna be okay."

Mrs. Pangbourn nodded. "Atta boy, Matt. Call me if you want to talk." She raised an eyebrow. "Ross has the number." And I grinned.

She turned to my mom, asking a bunch of questions about life with five kids. While they yakked, I planted my elbows on my knees and leaned forward a little. I took one last look at the greatest photograph ever to hold down a stack of papers on a principal's desk—that amazing team picture with Lisa Lewis in the middle holding up a championship trophy and smiling faintly. Looking about the same age back then as Tom was now.

You know, too bad Lisa Lewis was a girl and had to dink around with softball. With all that talent, she could have turned pro. But instead of turning pro, Lisa had turned into Mrs. Pangbourn, amateur baseball coach and professional middle school principal. Things had worked out for her. Maybe not great, because nobody in her right mind would voluntarily hang around middle school for the rest of her life, no matter what it paid. Still, Mrs. Pangbourn looked happy, third-place finish and all.

Happy. I looked down at my hands, folded between my knees. Happy was more than I could ask for. But I figured I could look up and feel the sun on my face sometimes and be okay with it. Okay, no matter what happened.

I turned my wrists a little until my empty palms faced up. I watched them move up and down. A balance scale. Dread in one hand and hope in the other. It was like hitting a double and then stealing third on two outs. You wait there, standing deep on the third-base line, a little heartsick that after all that struggle, all that pain, you might not get hit home. Still, there was no denying it. There my brother was, holding at third. It was another real pretty day.